The Sunita Experiment

Mitali Perkins

The Sunita Experiment

SCHOLASTIC INC.

New York   Toronto   London   Auckland   Sydney
Mexico City   New Delhi   Hong Kong

Copyright © 1993 by Mitali Perkins.
All rights reserved. Published by Scholastic Inc., 555 Broadway, New York, NY 10012, by arrangement with Little, Brown and Company Inc., 1271 Avenue of the Americas, New York, NY 10020.
SCHOLASTIC and associated logos and designs are trademarks and/or registered trademarks of Scholastic Inc.

Printed in the U.S.A.

ISBN 0-439-22954-5

3 4 5 6 7 8 9 10   23   08 07 06 05 04 03

For my Dadu

Acknowledgments

My first book makes it to the finish line with loud cheers, faithful prayers, and constant encouragement. Much of the cheerleading and praying in my life is done by Mom and Dad Perkins, "Gaga" (Mrs. Estelle Chapman), my sisters, Rupali Hofmann and Sonali McElroy, and their husbands, Rev. Carl Hofmann and Alan McElroy.

Two writing friends, Elizabeth Lund and Laura Brittain, read early versions and said, "Pursue it," when I wasn't sure. Megan Tingley of Joy Street Books made my first taste of working with an editor an extremely enjoyable one.

For my first twenty-three years, my beloved mom and dad, Sailendra Nath and Madhusree Bose, provided the daily encouragement needed to motivate a would-be writer who would much rather read than buckle down and write. In 1986, they agreed to share the job with my husband, Rev. Robert Kincaid Perkins II.

With the single-minded dedication that characterizes everything he does, Rob took up the challenge and added his own distinctive flourish. He listens. He edits. He talks and thinks about the characters and dilemmas as though they were people in our church or neighborhood. But more than all of that, he teaches me about fresh starts and loyal love, two themes I seek to weave into my writing. And he knows my heart's desire—that everything I do, including writing, will please and honor our dearest Friend, the one who gave his life for us.

The Sunita Experiment

Chapter 1

Sunita slammed her locker shut. She was going to be late to social studies, but she desperately needed some time alone. Liz would save her a seat. Bathroom stalls were the only private places in the entire junior high school. She needed some toilet tissue anyway, to blow her nose.

When Ingrid Bergman cried, thought Sunita, tears glistened glamorously in her eyes. Streams of water certainly never came gushing out of her nose. Sunita had discovered the movie *Casablanca* a few weeks ago. She loved the black-and-white World War II setting, Bergman's exotic Swedish accent, and, of course, Humphrey Bogart sitting gloomily in a dark, smoky corner.

In the girls' room, LeAnn Schaeffer and Jeannie Adams were laughing together in front of the mirror. Jeannie was putting on lipstick, and LeAnn had

3

her purse-size bottle of styling mousse in one hand and a hairbrush in the other. They stopped giggling when Sunita came in.

"Hi, Sunni," said Jeannie, after an awkward pause.

"Hi," mumbled Sunita as she hurried past them.

LeAnn gave her blond bangs one last brush. "Come on, Jeannie. We shouldn't be too late."

Just late enough to make an entrance, thought Sunita, leaning against the door of the stall to keep it closed. Of all the people to see. LeAnn Schaeffer. Michael's new girlfriend. The thought hurt even though she knew it wasn't true . . . yet.

Michael Morrison was the whole reason that she was in this stinky stall anyway. And late for class on the second day of school. Michael had walked by her in the hall again without saying a word—he'd deliberately looked away. They hadn't talked in a week. And somehow LeAnn had managed to attach herself to him, pulling him into her intimate circle of the most popular kids in the eighth grade.

Sunita's first romance, foiled by the arrival of an airplane from a distant shore. She cheered up a little. Bergman and Bogart's romantic good-bye in *Casablanca* had also been plane related.

She stuffed yards of toilet paper into her purse in case her nose betrayed her in the middle of class. A long, private cry in her own room was in order, she decided. And then she remembered that she didn't have her own room anymore. *They* had taken

4

it. The Wright brothers should never have invented the airplane. They should have foreseen the untold damage it would cause in the future. Especially in the thwarted life of Sunita Sen.

On her way out, she gave the mirror her best attempt at a seductive but innocent look. In every scene of *Casablanca*, Ingrid Bergman's face left men entranced with its beauty. Sunita sighed in disappointment. A round, basically cheerful face was just not designed to allure. Even in the throes of heartbreak, it looked as if it had been tailor-made to fit the name her first-grade teacher had given her— Sunny, or Sunni. Of course the name had stuck.

And there was just nothing particularly entrancing about the rest of her. Medium weight. Medium height. Brown eyes, dark skin. Shoulder-length, straight black hair. If only she could wear a little lipstick. But Dad said thirteen was way too young for makeup. Even though every other girl in the eighth grade wore it. Oops. Almost every other girl. She'd forgotten about Liz.

Liz had been Sunita's best friend since the first grade. But lately she had become another item on Sunita's list of top ten worries. Liz always had her nose in a book. She actually enjoyed schoolwork and didn't care if people knew it. And she still thought of boys as her buddies—when she thought about them at all. Romance and Liz were like a pair of mismatched socks. Absolutely useless together.

This year Sunita had vowed to do something about it. If she wasn't careful, she and Liz might have to join the infamous group of Strange Kids and Social Rejects who spent their lunch hour watching old *Star Trek* videos in the library.

She peeked in through the pane of glass on the door. She hated to walk in late and have everybody look up and stare at her. The class was divided into current events groups, discussing articles Mr. Riley had clipped from the *Chronicle*. Liz was deep in a heated discussion with Kevin Chang. Her curly red hair was tousled and her glasses askew as she waved the article in the air to make a point. Sunita slipped into the seat beside her friend.

You'd think Liz would take advantage of a sister like Traci, she thought. Liz's sister Traci was . . . dazzling. A mane of blond hair cascading down her back. Clothes right out of *Cosmopolitan* magazine. A gang of swarthy guys lurking around the Graysons' house, trying to catch a glimpse of her.

"I like to live on the edge of danger," she'd told Sunita once.

If only Sunita had a sister like that—someone who would have worn Mom and Dad down a bit. Instead, she had Sangita—or Geetie, as everyone called her—who put even more obstacles in her path. This past summer, Geetie had been furious at Sunita for shaving her legs. She'd delivered one of her famous feminist speeches when she'd found the razor.

Geetie was eighteen and in her first year of college at Berkeley. She wore her hair long and parted in the middle with no bangs. Her typical outfit was a Peruvian alpaca sweater over jeans. Two or three Indian scarves draped around her neck. African earrings. And Mexican huaraches. No traditional dates for Geetie—just political discussions or poetry readings over coffee in one of Berkeley's dark coffeehouses. And to her, makeup was a symbol of male dominance—as well as a waste of natural resources. She'd probably spend her life uniting all the tribal women in the world in one huge recycling project or something.

Suddenly, Sunita realized that Mr. Riley was standing in front of her desk. "Sunita Sen, right?" he asked.

Sunita nodded and took the colored tacks he handed her. She could already tell Mr. Riley was going to be a deadly, consciousness-raising type of teacher. Yesterday, he'd pinned a *National Geographic* map of the world on the bulletin board. Each kid had been asked to find out where they had "roots." And now he was handing out colored tacks. Not a good sign, thought Sunita, watching as he rolled up his sleeves, sat on his desk, and clapped his hands to get their attention. Not a good sign at all.

"Take your tacks and stick them on the map over your places of ancestry," he announced, when the class quieted down.

As one classmate after another put their tacks on the map, Europe got more and more crowded, and Sunita felt more and more apprehensive.

Then Ilana Taylor's turn came. Ilana was black, tall, and slender. At thirteen, she'd already started modeling in local fashion shows. Her pin went proudly onto Angola, in the southern part of Africa.

"We don't really know where we come from originally," she said. "But my dad thinks his great-grandfather must have been born somewhere near Angola. Before he lived in Alabama, that is."

She shoved her other tack onto the southern United States and strode gracefully back to her seat.

The class shifted uncomfortably. Nobody said anything. The kid who was next put his tacks on Germany and England with an uneasy look on his face.

Kevin Chang, who'd been in Sunita's class since the second grade, went next and stuck his lone tack on the huge country of China.

"That's me. One hundred percent purebred," he announced to the class. "You guys are just a bunch of mutts."

The class snickered nervously.

Sunita's turn came and she, too, put only one tack on the map—right on Calcutta, India. Her eyes swept over the distance between India and Poland, where John Rostowski had put the pin nearest to hers. Even Kevin's pin seemed far away, high up in the northernmost province of China.

Finally, Mr. Riley stuck his own tacks on Ireland and England.

"Together, Sunita's, Ilana's, and Kevin's tacks represent two-thirds of the world's population," he told the class. "Despite what we see in our neighborhood, most of the world does not have white skin and European roots."

As Mr. Riley went on, Sunita stared down at her desk. *He would have to single me out on the first week of school,* she thought. She would have given anything for Michael to turn in his chair and smile his crinkly grin at her. He would have if their friendship hadn't come crashing to an end. And she knew exactly when it had crashed. She could pinpoint the time to the minute.

It was when her grandparents had arrived from India one week ago. Only one week. But it seemed like forever to Sunita. She'd never forget it.

It had been like a scene from a bad movie. The whole family—Sunita, her parents, Geetie, and Ajit, or A.J., who'd driven to the airport from Stanford University—watched and waved from behind the glass that overlooked the international arrivals and customs area. Her grandfather wore a traditional white dhoti—a long piece of cotton cloth wrapped around his waist and legs. Her grandmother clutched her husband with one hand and a bag of mangoes with the other. Mangoes were her son-in-law's favorite fruit. The customs officer patiently, and then not so patiently, explained why she couldn't bring fresh fruit from another country into America.

Finally, they got through customs. And sometime during all the tears and embracing, Mom had stopped being *her* mother and had changed into being *their* daughter right in front of Sunita's eyes.

"Sunni. Sunni! What do you think about the issue?" Liz interrupted Sunita's train of thought with a warning look. They were supposed to be back in their discussion groups, and Mr. Riley had come over to watch their group. He expected all of them to participate and said he would grade them accordingly. Sunita rallied, but could only come up with this fairly standard I-was-too-paying-attention decoy response:

"Well, I agree with you, Liz, on your last point," she said, leaning forward in her chair. "But maybe Kevin should explain his point of view one more time so that we all understand it better."

A feeble but valiant try. It could be early enough in the year to fool Mr. Riley, but somehow Sunita didn't think so. She could swear he stifled a smile as he left to spy on another group.

Chapter 2

"Let's go to your house, Liz," Sunita called out over the noise.

They pushed their way past kids and bags and musical instruments to their seat in the back of the bus. One of the privileges of being in the eighth grade was the respectful way seventh-graders stayed away from the seats claimed by eighth-graders.

"I'm sick of my house," complained Liz. "Traci's lovesick men are always hanging around. Besides, track practice starts next week, and then I'll never get to visit you. Your house is so exciting since your grandparents came. And your mom might have some leftover curry for me." Her eyes lit up. She loved hot food.

"Exciting? Hah!" Sunita snorted, pushing open the window. The September day was as warm as summer, although the days were getting shorter.

11

An Indian summer, in more ways than one. The pun made her wince.

"I think it's exciting. Besides, your grandmother asked me to help her learn American." Liz took out a bag of tortilla chips from her huge shoulder bag and offered one to Sunita. Although she was constantly eating, the nickname that Bill McTaggart—another one of LeAnn's groupies—had given her still fit. "The Stick," he called her. Liz didn't care. She called him "the Goon" right to his face.

"There's no such language as 'American,' silly," answered Sunita.

"Your grandmother says there is. Anyway, I want to see your mom. She's been wearing those beautiful dresses every day since your grandparents came."

Sunita flinched. When Liz was enthusiastic about something, her voice took on a booming, joyful quality. And LeAnn and Michael were just two seats in front of them. She lowered her own voice, hoping Liz would get the message. "They're not dresses, Liz. They're called sarees. Yards and yards of cloth that she has to wrap around herself."

Mom had never worn sarees before *they* arrived. She'd taught chemistry at the local junior college in tailored suits and blouses. But now she was on leave to stay home with her parents during their year-long visit. And she wore sarees every day to make *them* feel more at home.

"But you're more comfortable in jeans!" Sunita had protested. "It's more you."

"That's not true, Bontu," her mom had answered. Bontu—which meant "Little Sister"—was Sunita's pet name at home. And only at home. The family was under strict orders never to call her anything but Sunita when other people were around. Except Liz, of course, who'd been coming to their house since the first grade.

"Sarees are very comfortable," her mom had continued. "Besides, it makes your grandparents happy to see I haven't changed that much, and I think it makes your old-fashioned dad happy too."

"There is nothing as lovely and graceful on a woman as a saree," her dad said, peering over his newspaper to admire the green silk one his wife was wearing.

Sunita sighed. Dad was hopelessly stuck in his ways. But she'd expected more from Mom. When Michael had begun to come over in the summer, Mom hadn't once called Sunita by her pet name. She and Michael would play Ping-Pong downstairs, and Mom would bring them a plate of cookies. And then she'd leave, after just the right amount of small talk, carefully calling her daughter "Sunita" the whole time.

But it had been Mom, not Dad, who'd told her not to invite boys over while her grandparents were visiting. Sunita got angry all over again at the memory.

"That's so fake, Mom!" she'd said accusingly. "Why can't we do what we always do?"

"It's just for a little while," Mom had said, looking away. "Just until they get a bit more used to the culture."

She was mad at Mom for being so wishy-washy, but at the same time she was secretly relieved. Her grandmother and grandfather were so . . . different. And Michael was so . . . well, so *normal.*

Look at the way her grandmother pinched Liz's cheeks when Liz came over. Liz was thirteen, for heaven's sake. Too big for cheek pinching. She'd die if her grandmother pinched Michael's cheek or patted him on the head. Liz was different—she'd been around for ages. There was no way Sunita was going to let Michael meet her grandparents, and Mom's request only made things easier.

The bus drove past the wide lawns and big houses in Michael's neighborhood. She'd visited him there once in a while during the summer, but she knew he preferred going to her house.

The day after her grandparents had moved in, Sunita had met Michael at the park. They'd sat on a bench by the tennis courts, watching what seemed like hundreds of little kids squealing and tossing water balloons at any sign of life.

"This is crazy. Every kid in the neighborhood is here," Michael had said. "Let's go to your house, Sunni."

"My house is so small," she'd answered, trying to keep her voice casual. "And now it feels so crowded."

"With your grandparents here, you mean? We can always go downstairs and play Ping-Pong. Besides, I'm craving your mom's munchies."

"Uh . . . I'm kind of busy for the rest of the day, Michael. I've got to go home and get stuff ready for school."

"What do you have to get ready for the first day?" And then he'd turned and looked into her eyes. "What's wrong, Sunni? You're sure acting funny. Don't you want me to come over?"

She'd felt cornered. She couldn't tell him that Mom had asked her not to bring boys to the house. It made the Sen family seem as though they belonged to another century. Or maybe a different planet.

She looked down, quiet. Eventually, the silence got uncomfortable.

"That's okay," he'd said finally, his voice low. "I can take a hint."

He'd even waited a bit. Giving her one more chance. But she hadn't said anything. And then he'd walked away.

Out of Sunita's life forever. Never to speak to or

see each other again. *Until one day, when their eyes meet across a smoky, dimly lit café. Soft piano music is playing. She is wearing a slinky evening dress, and—*

"Ah—Ah—AH—CHOO!"

A loud, forceful, and disgustingly wet-sounding sneeze rocketed from the seat behind her.

"Yuck!" she said, turning around. "Can't you use a tissue?"

It was a seventh-grader. One of the three squirts who usually sat squashed together in the undesirable seat over the back tire. Today his seatmates were avoiding whatever infectious disease had exploded onto the back of Sunita's head.

"Adder-jees," he whispered apologetically, accepting the toilet paper she shoved at him.

Sunita went back to her thoughts. Maybe she was being a little too melodramatic about all of this separation stuff. All those hours she'd spent watching *Casablanca* had gone to her head. Michael was in three of her classes and was a fellow member of the Honor Society. They had to ride the same school bus every day. At some point, he was going to have to talk to her again.

She hadn't told Liz how she felt about Michael. Liz had been at science camp all summer when Sunita and Michael had started spending more time together. She would think Sunita was crazy, anyway. They'd all been in the same class since the first

16

grade. Liz would bring up some horrible story about pudgy little elementary-school Michael. She probably still thought of him like that, even though he'd become one of the most popular guys in the whole school.

Michael—the tall and lean eighth-grade Michael with gorgeous brown eyes and blond hair—got off the bus. Sunita noted with some satisfaction that LeAnn stayed on.

"How come you don't feel like going home?" asked Liz, breaking into her thoughts.

"I don't even feel like it is home anymore," Sunita grumbled. "Not since I had to move into Geetie's room."

She looked at Liz's disappointed face.

"Okay, okay. Since you're obviously going through Indian food withdrawal, we'll go to my house. Happy?"

Liz nodded, beaming. She returned to her book. Sunita glanced at it with hope. She had checked out *The Teenager's Bible of Beauty Basics* from the library a while ago and had casually left it in Liz's room.

But no. *Beauty Basics* was accruing overdue charges in a corner somewhere. Liz was reading *The Lion, the Witch and the Wardrobe*. Again.

"Elizabeth Anne Grayson! How many times have you read that book?" Sunita asked.

"This makes seventeen." Liz didn't even look up

to answer. She was already far away, rediscovering the magic wardrobe with Peter, Susan, Edmund, and Lucy.

Sunita groaned. She had to admit that her old copy of *The Secret Garden* was great company on rainy days. But only Liz would read the same kids' book seventeen times. Only Liz would know it was the seventeenth time she was reading it. And only Liz would read it on the school bus for one and all to see.

Chapter 3

You could smell the spices sizzling as soon as you walked in—garlic and cumin, onion and turmeric. When Michael visited over the summer, Sunita hurried him downstairs before his nose had a chance to get assaulted. Liz, on the other hand, started sniffing like a puppy and followed the smells into the kitchen.

Sunita stopped in the living room to turn down the volume on the stereo. She had heard the Indian music playing half a block away—twanging sitar music that grated on her nerves and made their house sound like a mecca for aging hippies. A grumpy neighbor had already complained three times since Sunita's grandparents had arrived.

Squinting, her hands on her hips, she tried to see their house through Michael's eyes. Too cluttered. Those paisley prints clashed. Too many batiks on

19

the wall and plants in baskets. And way too many pictures of too many relatives.

Mrs. Morrison, Michael's mom, had just redecorated her house. Clean linen furniture accented by soft splashes of teal and peach pillows. Empty white walls with simple etchings of seashells and sailboats. Huge stretches of spotless white carpet. A baby grand piano, gleaming with wax and perpetually tuned.

Sunita sighed and picked up the incense holder from the coffee table. The incense stick had burned itself down to a pile of ashes.

In the kitchen, Mom was stirring something at the stove. Liz was happily eating a *samosa*—a pocket of bread stuffed with curried potatoes and onions. Sunita's grandmother squatted on a small stool, singing loudly with the music. A sharp curved blade attached to a piece of wood and a basket were on the floor between her feet. Holding a chili pepper between the thumb and forefinger of both hands, she pushed it against the blade. Her fingers moved quickly. The blade flashed through the pepper and pieces of the chili fell into the basket.

Sunita dumped the ashes from the incense holder into the garbage can. "Why can't she use a knife and cutting board instead of that thing?" she asked her mother.

Mom glanced over to make sure Sunita's grandmother hadn't heard. "She's not used to a knife,

Bontu," she whispered. "That 'thing' is normal for her."

Mom's face was flushed from standing over the sizzling frying pan. Soft wisps of hair that were too short to be pulled into her French braid curled around her face. And her eyes—Mom's eyes were big and brown and framed by long lashes. Dad always said that when he saw her for the first time, her eyes had stolen his heart. But lately, there were tiny new lines around Mom's eyes. As Sunita watched, Mom wiped her hot face with the end of the faded cotton saree she was wearing.

Mom's tailored suits and silk shirts were hanging in an ordered row in her closet, wrapped in shrouds of dry-cleaner's bags. Her leotards and aerobics tights lay neatly folded in drawers. They used to lie tangled together on top of the dryer, waiting for Mom to grab one of them to wear to her aerobics class. Mom hadn't worked out in ages, Sunita realized. The month before *they* got here, she'd been too busy getting the house spotless. And now she was too busy keeping it that way.

She frowned at the pile of *samosa* on her friend's plate, realizing that Mom was still wearing that red dot on her forehead and a stripe of red powder on the part in her hair. Sunita had started to complain the first time Mom had worn the red dot and stripe— when they were about to go to the airport.

"Do you have to wear that dumb dot on the middle

21

of your forehead, Mom? And what is that red stuff on your head? It looks just like blood!"

"The stripe is to show everyone that I'm married, Bontu," Mom had answered. "Just like a wedding ring. Your grandmother wears one too. And the dot is just like makeup. It's designed to draw attention to the eyes."

Dad had given her one of his stern looks. "Your mom is excited to see her parents, Bontu," he'd said, pulling her aside. "It's been ten years since she's seen them, and she's a little nervous. Don't make this any tougher on her."

Sunita's impatient remarks subsided, though she still grumbled under her breath. But now she wished she hadn't given in so easily. Mom had worn the dot, stripe, and saree every day since then. And she had been right—they certainly drew attention.

Just last night, Mom and Sunita had gone shopping. At the drugstore, the middle-aged saleswoman came out from behind the counter to admire Mom's saree. A couple of Mom's aerobics friends, still sweaty from their workout, joined in the *ooh*s and *aah*s. Mom was too busy to notice the group of elementary-school kids staring and giggling.

"Hey, you guys," one of them said. "That lady's got the evil eye on her forehead. Let's get out of here before we get cursed!"

Laughing and screeching, they had run out of

the store and down the street. Sunita had escaped to the car, vowing never to be seen with Mom until she looked normal again.

"Ah . . . AH . . . HELP!" Liz's scream echoed through the house.

Sunita jumped up. Her friend had accidentally bitten into a hefty chunk of chili pepper, and sweat beads were pouring down her forehead. Sunita filled a glass with water and popped a couple of ice cubes in it. With a grateful look, Liz stopped panting long enough to drink the whole glass.

"Where's Dadu, Aunty?" she asked over the piece of ice she was rolling on her tongue. Indian kids call their friends' parents "Uncle" and "Aunty." Liz had been calling Mom "Aunty" since the first grade. Before Sunita's grandparents arrived, Mom had taught Liz the Bengali words for grandfather and grandmother that Sunita, Geetie, and A.J. used— "Dadu" for grandfather and "Didu" for grandmother.

"Dadu's in the back yard," Mom answered. "He's going to attack that back yard and plant a whole new garden for the spring. Which reminds me—I had a great idea today."

She turned to her daughter with a hopeful look that made Sunita immediately suspicious.

"What idea?" asked Liz, not noticing Sunita's frown.

"I thought maybe you girls could help him. It would be a great chance to learn about gardening . . ."

Mom's voice trailed off as she looked at her daughter standing with her chin out and arms folded across her chest.

Liz sighed. "I wish I could, but track practice starts next week."

"Track . . . track . . . track . . . What is this *track*?" asked Didu.

Sunita winced at her grandmother's thick Indian accent. Bergman's Swedish accent in *Casablanca* sounded so . . . cultured. Why couldn't the Sens have been from France or Belgium or someplace that produced sophisticated accents?

Didu had been studying English in India and was excited to show off her proficiency in America. Unfortunately, she'd learned right away that her formal language and strong accent made it tough for Americans to understand her. Refusing to be discouraged, she had decided to "learn American." She zealously pounced on any new word and rolled it around in her mouth like a hungry frog devouring a tasty fly.

"Track is a sports event, Didu," Liz explained slowly, so that the older woman could hear how she pronounced the word. "I run races for my school. One mile and two miles."

"Such a big girl running for fun? When I was

your age, my parents were already inviting suitors to the house for tea."

"Suitors? *Yuck!*" answered Liz with a grimace. "Just the thought of them would help me run faster."

"Yuck. Yuck. Yuck . . . What is this *yuck*?"

Sunita tried to imagine her friend serving tea to a prospective husband the way Indian girls did. She caught Mom's eyes in the old understanding amusement for a moment.

"Hey, Sunni, I just had a great idea!" Liz said, when she was sure Didu could use her newest American word properly. "You could help Dadu and do your observation experiment for science class at the same time!"

Sunita tried to flash Liz a be-quiet-or-I'll-kill-you look, but it was too late.

"What experiment?" asked Mom.

"We have to set something constant as a control group, and then set up three other groups exactly like the first with only one thing changed in each one. Then all semester long we keep a notebook with detailed observations about the whole experiment. Like Sunita can plant something as her control plant, and then change the amount of water it gets or something, and—"

"Mom knows what an experiment is," interrupted Sunita. "She used to be a chemistry teacher, remember."

Mom ignored Sunita's emphasis on the words

25

"used to be." "It would be a good place to do your experiment, Bontu," she said.

"I'll think about it," Sunita mumbled. "Come on, Liz. We have tons of homework. Let's go downstairs."

Sunita knew that they wouldn't be interrupted there. Her grandparents tiptoed around the house when Sunita or Geetie was studying.

Didu got up from the stool and tucked the front of her saree more securely into her petticoat. "You should see how your cousins in Calcutta study," she said in Bengali to Sunita. "Day and night they bend over their books. And when the power goes out, Shefali burns a kerosene lamp late into the night."

Sunita could understand Bengali, although she always answered in English. "I wish Shefali could take this math test for me" was all she said now.

"Thanks a lot," she said to Liz, as the girls headed downstairs. "The last thing I want to do is spend time after school working in the garden with my grandfather."

Liz was juggling her book bag and a huge basket full of snacks. "I don't know what's gotten into you lately, Sunni. I think it's a great idea."

"What do you know? Your family's so normal," said Sunita, plopping down on the pile of big pillows in the family room. "And I'm already so sick of stories about our wonder-cousins in Calcutta. 'Shefali would *never* wear such a short dress in public, Tara's hair is *so* much longer and thicker than yours, Jai's

26

been at the top of *his* class since kindergarten,' and so on and so on."

"Can't you see your grandma's just like mine? You know, kind of braggy and proud about her grand-kids in front of everyone except whoever she's brag-ging about. I bet Shefali and what's-her-name will get sick of Sunita stories when Didu and Dadu go back."

She grabbed a handful of cookies. "I'm going out to say hello to Dadu. Whom I happen to enjoy spending time with," she announced.

Sunita thought about what Liz had said. Didu did rave about Geetie's brains and straight A's when Geetie wasn't around. But as soon as Geetie came home, the girls would hear stories starring their "pretty, sweet, and feminine" cousin Mina, who was just about Geetie's age. "Mina feminina," Geetie had christened her after an especially vivid description of the flowers Mina had worn in her lustrous, long black hair during a dance recital.

Liz came back with her hands full of tiny green apples. The cookies had disappeared.

"Right off the tree—yum!" she said. "Did you know that Dadu played on the cricket team in col-lege? He told me all about cricket. See, one guy is the pitcher—"

"We've got a math quiz tomorrow, Liz. Remem-ber? We don't have time to discuss some dumb Indian game," said Sunita.

27

"For your information, Miss Sunita Sen, cricket is played in almost every other country in the world except here," said Liz. "But you're right. I hear Mr. Ogden's math quizzes are killers."

After an hour of studying and munching on apples, peanuts, and more cookies, Liz got up to stretch and pack her bag.

"I'm starved," she said, looking at her watch. "It's almost time for dinner. Don't forget to ask if you can spend the night on Friday. I still don't get why you want to go to Traci's party. I had a terrible time convincing Traci. She said that we absolutely have to be upstairs by ten-thirty, and we can't breathe a word about the party to Mom or Dad."

That was exactly why Sunita wanted to go. It was the perfect chance to learn what really went on at those wild parties Traci was always dropping hints about.

At the door, Liz stopped and turned around, twirling one of her curls around her finger the way she always did when she felt uncomfortable.

"What's up?" asked Sunita.

Staring fiercely at the lobelia in a planter on the porch, Liz blurted out swiftly, "I-don't-think-Michael-really-likes-LeAnn-I-saw-him-watching-you-on-the-bus-today-so-don't-worry-about-it-so-much-okay?''

She flashed a smile at Sunita before bounding away.

Sunita grinned and shut the door. That Liz! She deserved more credit. If she was right about Michael, maybe there was still hope.

She is wearing a beautifully tailored Pierre Cardin suit and veiled hat, and her profile looks strangely like an Indian version of Ingrid Bergman's. A lean Bogart-like man (who has Michael's gorgeous brown eyes) leans forward in his seat to stare intently, wondering when he'd seen that tilt of chin before, those mysterious dark eyes, the pearl earrings—

"Bon-tu!" Mom called from the kitchen.

Mentally clothing herself in a crisply ironed suit, silky hose, and high-heeled pumps, Sunita glided into the kitchen. She practiced Ingrid Bergman's small, sad smile of mystery behind an imaginary veil, as Didu handed her the vegetable peeler.

"You used to smile like that when you were a baby," said Didu. "What a chubby and jolly baby you were!"

Sunita sighed. Her grandmother pinched her cheek and swatted her on the back of her Pierre Cardin.

Chapter 4

"You look a little tired, Mom," Sunita said, when dinner was simmering and the kitchen tidied up. "You rest. I'll give Dad his tea."

"Thanks, Bontu," answered Mom. "I do have a bit of a headache. I think I'll rest for a few minutes."

Resting for a few minutes was something Mom had been doing more and more. Sunita felt a twinge of guilt as Mom smiled a grateful smile and headed off to her bedroom. She wanted Mom out of the way for a reason.

When the Sen kids wanted permission for something, they all knew that the best strategy was to approach their mother first. Lately, though, Mom had been referring everything to Dad without any discussion. And Sunita knew where Dad stood on the issue of sleeping over at friends' houses.

But Sunita wasn't the youngest for nothing. All three of them knew that a rested and well-fed father was much easier to manage than a weary, neglected father. Diplomacy wins the day, Sunita told herself, remembering how Geetie and A.J. had coached her in approaching Dad for permission.

When she heard the garage door open, Sunita moved her backpack from its usual after-school roost on her dad's favorite chair. Then she hurried downstairs and grabbed her dad's briefcase. As usual, it was overflowing with letters and reports he hadn't had time to read at the office. Sunita's dad was an architect who specialized in earthquake-proofing buildings, which kept him busy in downtown San Francisco.

"Welcome home, Dad!" she said brightly, ignoring his raised eyebrows. "Today's mail is by your chair. I'll bring you some tea right away."

While Dad glanced through the mail and chatted with Didu, Sunita poured him a cup of tea and zapped a *samosa* in the microwave. She tried to think of a way to get her grandmother out of the room. Sunita and Geetie had agreed that Didu and Dad united would be almost unbeatable in any "discussion."

When Sunita entered the living room, she noticed with relief that Didu was concentrating on the comics, which she claimed helped her to "learn

American." Let's get this over with before she catches on to what's happening, Sunita thought. She handed her father his tea and *samosa*.

"By the way, Liz asked me to spend the night on Friday," she said. "Is it okay if I go?"

Dad put down the mail and looked up with a frown. Didu put down her paper and looked up with a frown. Even though she'd expected it, Sunita felt herself get irritated.

"You've only let me spend the night at Liz's house three times in my entire life," she told her father. "And that was only because you and Mom were out of town. When I think of all the slumber parties I've had to miss! The other girls think we're the weirdest family in the whole world."

"You know I don't care what all the other girls think. You have a perfectly good bed here in our house. I don't know why you need to sleep under someone else's roof."

"I don't need to. I *want* to. And besides, you're not being fair. What about Geetie and A.J.? Geetie's stayed at Berkeley a couple of nights, and A.J. doesn't even live here anymore."

"*You're* not being fair. Ajit has to live on campus. It was really hard on Mom and me when he left, but now we're getting used to it. And you know Geetie stays with the Banerjees only if she has a late chem lab and an early class the next morning. But other than that, we do expect her to be in her own bed."

Sunita groaned. "It sounds like you want us to live with you forever!"

Her dad smiled. "I know it doesn't make sense to you, Bontu. But in India, children do stay with their parents until they get married—"

He was interrupted by his mother-in-law.

"That I should live to see this day! One of *my* granddaughters actually begging to stay at another family's house!" She shook her head sorrowfully, as though Sunita's course down the slippery slope of rebellion was already predestined.

Sunita and her dad exchanged glances as Didu continued. "Arun, you know very well if your daughter sleeps at another house, it brings shame to the whole family. She is announcing to the world that she prefers somebody else's home and family to her own."

Maybe I do prefer somebody else's home and family to my own, Sunita thought, but she stopped herself before the words came tumbling out. Ignoring her grandmother, she moved behind her dad's chair and put her arms around him.

"We're not in India anymore, Dad. And the Graysons are just like relatives, aren't they?" she asked softly. "You know how you're always saying that Liz is more like an Indian girl than an American girl."

33

Liz's model behavior was Sunita's trump card. And Mrs. Grayson was one of Mom's closest friends.

Her dad sighed. "I guess you're right. We aren't in India anymore, as your brother and sister have done their best to remind me. It just feels strange that my baby won't be sleeping under my roof. But since we do know the Graysons so well . . ."

"Thanks, Dad," she whispered, giving him a big kiss on the cheek.

Didu sniffed loudly in her corner of the room, and Dad's frown came back. "Don't whisper when other people are in the room, Bontu," he said gruffly. "It's not polite."

"What's not polite?" Mom asked, coming into the room with a Stanford sweatshirt draped over her shoulders. Sunita's parents took a walk at the same time every evening, wearing their matching sweatshirts, sharing one umbrella if it rained.

Dad's face lost its frown as his wife came in. His eyes filled with pleasure as he watched her walk toward them, her saree flowing in graceful lines around her slim figure.

"A sweatshirt over a saree?" asked Sunita. "Looks kind of tacky to me. Not that I'm the expert on Indian fashion."

Didu eyed her daughter critically. "What is this *tacky,* I do not know," she said. "But that sweatshirt does not match. Take one of your pretty cardigans."

Mom stopped smiling and looked down at the

34

sweatshirt. It was her favorite. A.J. had brought one to each of his parents on his first visit home from Stanford. Slowly, she pulled it off her shoulders, but Dad stopped her.

"These sweatshirts were not given so that we would make a fashion statement. They were given so that everyone who sees us will know we belong together," said Dad. He grabbed his own sweatshirt from the closet, draped it over his shoulders, and escorted Mom out of the house.

Sunita escaped into the kitchen before Didu could remember the rest of her lecture. She sat down by the phone and waited. After about ten minutes, the phone rang. Sunita picked it up.

"Hi, Geetie," she said. Her sister always called when Mom and Dad were safely out on their walk.

"Hey! How'd you know it was me? Pretty smart, Bontu."

"How late are you going to be tonight?" Sunita asked.

As usual, Geetie was talking too fast to hear her. "Listen, I'm going to be late tonight. Can you tell Mom and Dad for me? I just heard the most amazing lecture on deforestation, and a bunch of us are going to take the lecturer to dinner. I'll be home around eleven."

"What about your bike?"

Geetie rode her bike to the station and took the train to campus. She kept badgering Dad to join

35

her, citing statistics about the energy crisis and the growing smog problem in the San Francisco Bay Area. Dad was one of those park-and-ride people.

"Maria's got her parents' car. She'll give me a ride home. I can get a ride with Dad to the station in the morning."

"I guess it's nice to have a car every now and then," Sunita couldn't help saying. "Good thing Maria isn't as smog-conscious as you are."

Maria was Geetie's best friend. They'd gone through high school together, where everyone thought of shy Maria as Geetie's shadow.

"She's moving to campus and only drove today to haul a load of her stuff, O Smart One," said Geetie. "I'd never let her drive every day. Hey, I gotta go! Oh—tell Dadu I desperately need his help tomorrow on my bio exam."

Sunita hung up the phone, feeling a bit drained, as she always did after talking with Geetie.

Dadu was pouring a cup of tea with his back to her, but she could tell that he was smiling.

"Your sister is a very breathtaking young woman, is she not?" he asked. Breathtaking. The word was perfect for Geetie.

"I guess so." Sunita started to leave the room. "Oh—she said to tell you she needs help studying biology."

"Excellent. The study of life always intrigues me."

Her grandfather pulled back a kitchen chair for her. "Won't you stay for a chat, Bontu?" he asked.

"Can't right now. I have to finish up my homework before our evening session."

Before her grandparents had arrived, Sunita's mom and dad had told her that she would have to review her homework with her grandfather each night. He was curious to see how American schools taught the subjects he'd spent forty years teaching in India, and had written to ask if his granddaughter would do him this small favor. Sunita had grumbled but had started taking her homework to Dadu.

"Study well, then," Dadu said now. "I would not sway you from the call to acquire wisdom. Perhaps later we may visit?"

Sunita wondered if she would ever get used to her grandfather's formal English and singsong Indian accent. "Sure, Dadu, later," she said, slipping out of the kitchen as Didu came in.

Sunita grinned as she headed downstairs, knowing that Dadu was about to get a detailed summary of today's episode of *Endless Hope*. Didu had watched every single daytime soap opera the first week they'd arrived in the States. By the end of the week, she'd rejected all of them except for *Endless Hope*. Most of the main characters in *Endless Hope* were over fifty and kept their clothes on, although the love scenes were still slightly steamy in an old-fashioned way. Every evening, Dadu drank his tea and patiently listened to a recap of the day's show.

Sunita was discovering that she could snatch about an hour of freedom while this happened. Her parents seemed to be taking longer and longer walks, and Geetie was never home this early.

She popped *Casablanca* into the VCR and settled comfortably in her favorite (and forbidden) position—on her stomach two feet away from the television. Ingrid Bergman had just made a graceful, elegant entrance into Rick's café. . . .

Chapter 5

"**H**EY! WATCH IT!" Sunita yelled, as the kid behind her tripped and knocked her down the last steps of the bus.

Liz hurried to help her up.

"You okay, Sunni?" she asked, brushing her friend off.

Sunita's bag had flown open. Books and papers were strewn all around her. One of her palms was bleeding, and she'd torn a hole in the knee of her blue jeans. She pretended not to notice as LeAnn, Jeannie, and Michael got off the bus. Or that LeAnn and Jeannie were giggling.

"Gee . . . Gosh. I'm *so* sorry."

She turned around to see if she knew the culprit. Of course. It was the seventh-grader with allergies.

"My tuba case—it's kinda big and I can't really see over it—and my backpack straps kinda hang down, see . . ." His voice trailed off, and he started picking up her papers.

Liz repacked her bag while Sunita limped over to the water fountain to wash the blood off her hand.

"Here's your math book."

Sunita whirled around, banging her already bruised knee on the fountain. It was Michael, with LeAnn and Jeannie waiting behind him, still giggling. He handed her the book and turned away. Sunita swallowed.

"Michael!" she called.

He stopped. Turned around. "Yeah?"

"Thanks."

She watched as the crinkly grin spread across his face. It felt like forever since she'd seen it.

"You go to the nurse's office," he said. "We'll tell Mr. Riley you'll be late."

"Watch your step, Sunni," LeAnn called out sweetly. Two perfectly manicured fingers tugged firmly on the sleeve of Michael's jacket.

The nurse patched Sunita up, clucking and patting the way school nurses always do.

She is lying in a hospital bed, hearing Michael's voice calling her name. As she comes out of a deep sleep, she can make out the forms of two nurses, each holding huge bouquets of roses.

"There's no room for these," one nurse is whispering.

"He's already brought her five dozen. And he won't leave her bedside."

"Look at him," the other replies. *"He's been here for days—barely eating, full of remorse, saying her name over and over again. What's the use? She's not likely to make it through the night."*

"I want you to write a two-page report about marriage," Mr. Riley was telling the class when she limped in. As usual, the class groaned.

"Write about marriage in any non-European culture," Mr. Riley continued, ignoring them. "This film should get you thinking."

As Mr. Riley started the video called "Marriage and Family Rites of the Inuit," Sunita glanced over at Michael. LeAnn had moved to get a better view of the television, which of course meant she was much closer to Michael. As Sunita watched, she leaned over and whispered something in his ear. Her honey-blond hair gleamed in the dim light, and a few strands fell across Michael's shoulder. It was almost the same color as his.

They look as if they belong together, she thought. Like Bogart and Bergman. On the video, an Inuit family walked side by side across a wide expanse of ice. They seemed to belong together too.

Sometimes Sunita loved the rich darkness of her

skin—the color of caramel in the winter, the color of copper in the summer, the color everyone else coveted enough to bake for hours in the sun. But lately, she was aware of her skin in a new way. It didn't seem bronze or copper. It just seemed dark. Too dark.

"In Inuit culture, kinship networks are important," the narrator's voice droned. "Families must establish good relationships before an unmarried man and woman meet."

Sunita thought, What did the Morrisons' immaculate house, country club membership, and designer clothes have in common with the Sens? A kid in eighth grade. And that's about it.

On the screen, the Inuit husband and wife hid behind a fur and rubbed noses while their kids slept peacefully in another curve of the igloo. Outside, the sled dogs snuggled together for warmth.

When she got home from school, Sunita went into the kitchen. "Mom, can you tell me about Indian marriages? I have to write a report about it."

"Sorry, Bontu. I've got tons of errands and dinner to cook. Why don't you ask Dadu?"

Sunita turned away. Mom was so busy these days, cooking and cleaning. Why couldn't they just order a pizza the way they used to?

She rummaged through her drawers, found a pad of blank paper, and sharpened a couple of pencils. Sunita had loved to write ever since she was little. On rainy days, she leafed through her stack of old journals, chuckling over the poems and stories she'd written when she was seven or eight. She hadn't written all summer, she realized with a slight shock. She slipped a newly sharpened pencil behind her ear and went out to the back yard.

Gingerly, she picked her way past some nettles. Sunita's parents had always been too busy to plant a garden, and the weeds in the back yard had reigned unchallenged since the Sens had moved in. Hats off to Dadu for attacking this mess, Sunita thought. She couldn't imagine this wasteland ever becoming a garden.

Her grandfather was squatting beside one of the more jungly parts of the yard, singing to himself and pulling weeds. Sunita cleared her throat, and he looked up.

"Bontu!" he said, beaming. "What a pleasure to see you! Do you need some assistance with your studies?"

"Well, kind of," she answered. "I need to ask you some questions."

Her grandfather stood up and brushed the dirt off his hands.

"Let us make use of this elegant furniture, shall we?"

They made themselves comfortable on the rusty pieces of mismatched patio furniture that were scattered around the back yard.

"Now, how may I be of service?" he asked.

"Tell me how you and Didu met. You know, all the details and everything. I have to write an essay about Indian marriage customs, and I thought I could make it personal, so it's more interesting."

Dadu's eyes lit up behind his glasses.

"Ah, that's a story, all right. But interesting is not the word for it. Romantic, maybe. Or perhaps even passionate would better describe it."

Romantic? Passionate? Her thin, dignified grandfather and her plump grandmother? This she had to hear.

Her grandfather sat back in his chair and gazed off into the distance. The afternoon sun poured golden light over the hills behind the house.

" 'Although I conquer all the earth, yet for me there is only one city,' " he quoted, his voice low. " 'In that city there is for me only one house; and in that house, one room only; and in that room, a bed. And one woman sleeps there, the shining joy and jewel of all my kingdom.' "

He looked at Sunita. "A translation of a poem written in Sanskrit that leapt into my mind the first time I saw your grandmother."

She forgot all about the pad of paper and pencil

on her lap as she listened to his singsong voice describe the scene.

He has a good job and can even speak English. In India, speaking English means you can communicate with the British bosses and officers. It means power. His parents call a family council, and all the older, married relatives arrive. Each one carries envelopes, some with photos slipping out tantalizingly, some stacked neatly and tucked under an uncle's or aunt's arm.

He and his friends linger around the house and try to eavesdrop, but his mother comes out to shoo them away. They leave to play cricket with some of the other boys in the neighborhood, joking and laughing together.

One afternoon, his mother calls him in from the playing field.

"Take a bath and put on these clothes," she says, pointing to a fancy shirt and trousers laid out on the bed. He does as he is told. His parents are quiet as the three of them walk to the rickshaw stand. His stomach begins to feel jumpy as the rickshaw maneuvers over bumps and stones.

It stops in front of a house in another neighborhood. His mother looks him over and straightens his shirt collar. A man about his father's age comes out of the house and greets them. His father nudges him, and he bends to touch the man's feet and then his own forehead in the traditional greeting of honor given to older people. He does the same to several other people in the house and then sits close beside his father on a chair.

The conversation circles around him, and he glances around the room for clues. Pillows covered with delicate, colorful embroidery brighten up the simple furniture.

"Ah, he likes these pillows," says the most powdered and bejeweled woman of the lot. She has been watching his every move since they came in. "My sweet Ria knows how to sew most beautifully."

He gives her a polite smile and keeps his eyes on his knees, afraid to look anywhere else.

"Ria!" The lady's silk saree rustles as she goes to the door. "Bring in the tea, darling."

His parents sit up expectantly, but he keeps his eyes down. Feet stop before his father and mother, and a tea tray is lowered. He can't help noticing the feet— slender and graceful feet in rose-colored sandals that match the border of the saree covering the ankles. Underneath the saree, an ankle bracelet jingles softly. As the tea is poured, curiosity overwhelms him, and he looks up, forgetting that the room is quiet and that everybody is watching him.

Their eyes meet for a second, and then she looks quickly away. His heart is beating fast. The words of

the poem, memorized long ago in the privacy of his
room, jump unheralded into his mind.

His mother takes one look at his face and sits back
in her chair, satisfied.

"So when and how did you finally get married?" Sunita asked, when Dadu stopped talking. The shadows of the plum trees stretched across the jumble of weeds and wildflowers.

"When is your assignment due?" Dadu asked, glancing at her blank notepad.

"Not till Thursday."

"Then let us schedule another interview tomorrow afternoon, shall we? I must go upstairs and meet your grandmother for tea."

Sunita sat for a while after he left and counted the evening stars one by one as they appeared in the sky. I wonder if Michael drinks tea, she thought.

Chapter 6

When Mr. Riley handed the essays on marriage back to the class, he read Sunita's version of Dadu's story aloud. In the silence after he stopped reading, Sunita felt her cheeks get hot.

"You mean they only saw each other that one time and then they got married?" Ilana Taylor blurted out suddenly. Her classmates stared at her in surprise. Ilana usually spoke up only when the teacher directly asked her a question.

"Yup," answered Sunita. "Just once."

"How romantic," said Ilana.

"Romantic!" said LeAnn. "I think it's awful! I mean, to go home with someone you hardly know and have to sleep in the same bed with him! That's too gross!"

Whenever LeAnn talked, Sunni always pictured

it as part of a conversation in a book and felt an irrational surge of dislike for exclamation points. She pushed her feelings aside to mutter a quick prayer. Please God. Don't let Mr. Riley use this as one of his teachable moments. Let him read some-one else's essay.

But he was rolling up his shirtsleeves and sitting on his desk.

"What do some of you others think?" he asked.

About ten kids raised their hands.

"Go ahead, Liz," said Mr. Riley, picking the most energetically waving hand in the room.

"I think it's wonderful that they met only once be-fore their wedding day," Liz answered, giving LeAnn a quick look. "It's a lot better than people who know everything about each other before they get married and then get tired of each other after a few years."

Sunita was glad Liz had stood up for her, but she wished somebody else had spoken first. Liz was a bit too enthusiastic, and everybody knew they were best friends.

"Jeannie?" said Mr. Riley.

"I think it's terrible the way the parents arrange the whole thing. I mean, shouldn't people be free to choose who they want to marry?"

"Anybody want to answer that?"

No hands went up. Sunita tried to look engrossed in the cover of her social studies book.

"Okay, I'll take a stab at it," said Mr. Riley. "In this country, we value things like independence and freedom and individuality. In India, family and community are much more important. They don't think young people should have full responsibility for a decision that affects the whole family and generations to come."

"But Mr. Riley," interrupted Bill McTaggart, forgetting to raise his hand. "My doctor is Indian, and he was telling me that he and his wife met in college and got married."

"More and more people in India are moving to cities and becoming westernized," answered Mr. Riley. "But in the villages, it's still done much the way Sunita described. The interesting thing is that most Indians stay married for life. When times get tough, their society doesn't make it easy to back out of a commitment."

The class was quiet, thinking over what Mr. Riley had said. Over half had parents who were divorced or separated.

"I guess it's just a different way of doing it, that's all," said a voice from the back of the room, breaking the silence. Sunita felt her cheeks grow warm. Michael. Defending her honor. How gallant. What chivalry.

She looked up just in time to catch the look on LeAnn's face.

"I still think it's disgusting to have to sleep with

someone you don't even know!" LeAnn said to Jeannie, just loud enough for everyone around her to hear.

Liz jumped up from her seat, knocking her notebook onto the floor.

"Listen here, LeAnn Schaeffer," she said, putting one hand on her hip and waving her pencil in the air with the other. "Lots of times they wait a few months before they sleep together. They date after marriage. Sunni's grandfather used to bring his wife flowers and stuff every day for a whole year after they were married."

The bell rang.

"Okay, Liz, calm down," said Mr. Riley. "LeAnn is entitled to her opinion. I want all of you to give this some more thought."

Sunita grabbed Liz's arm and steered her over to their lockers. She had to make her friend understand that her intense loyalty only made things worse for them both.

"Liz—" she began.

"Okay, Sunni," Liz interrupted. "I'll admit I got carried away. But someone had to say something. I get so mad at that LeAnn Schaeffer."

She shut her locker and turned to face her friend. "How can you stand seeing her hang all over Michael like that? How come he lets that—that narrow-minded airhead cling to him like a leech?"

Sunita looked around her desperately. The halls

were full of their classmates heading off to second period. "Elizabeth Grayson!" she hissed. "Keep it down, will you?"

"I thought Morrison was smarter than that," Liz said, lowering her voice.

"I did too," Sunita admitted.

"What happened between the two of you anyway? You sure spent a lot of time together this summer. Your letters were full of 'Michael said so-and-so' and 'Michael and I did this-and-that.'"

Sunita sighed. "It's my abnormal family again. Mom asked me not to bring boys to the house because of *them*. Can you believe that?"

"Ohhh. She doesn't want to give Didu a major heart attack, right? But why would that make Morrison treat you differently?" Suddenly, the light dawned, and Liz grabbed Sunita's arm. "You didn't tell him the truth, did you, Sunni? He thinks you're not interested anymore, doesn't he?"

The tardy bell rang for second period. Liz hated to be late even more than Sunita did—not because everyone turned around to stare, but because she might miss some gem of knowledge that fell from the teacher's mouth.

"I'll come along, Liz. Save me a seat by the door," Sunita said, stopping by the girls' room.

"Don't you dare pretend you have to go to the bathroom, Sunita Sen. Look, I'll be the first to admit I'm no expert on romance, but I don't need Dear

Abby to give you some advice. Tell him the truth, Sunni. Give the guy some credit."

She slung her huge bag over her shoulder and glanced at her watch. "Enough tips to the lovelorn from Aunty Liz. I'm off like a herd of turtles!"

Liz careened down the hall, her bag bashing other tardy people right and left. Sunita followed slowly, thinking about her friend's advice. If she told Michael the truth, he would realize how incredibly different her family was from his. Or worse, he might actually come over some day when Mom relaxed a bit. A quick succession of images ran through her mind.

Didu, eating curry with her hands, asking Michael the meaning of every other word, and telling him the same stories over and over about the cousins in India. Dadu, squatting in the garden, his white linen dhoti knotted around his legs, reciting Bengali poetry to the soil and the seeds . . .

Sunita shuddered and made a firm resolution. The All-American Golden Boy would not darken the Sens' door until a plane with *them* in it had landed safely back in India. Even if it meant keeping her distance. Even if it meant the ultimate, unimaginable sacrifice.

Day and night he camped outside the convent on the banks of the moat, his eyes feverishly scanning the tiny windows, wondering if the rusty drawbridge would ever come down. Taking pity on him, a passerby told him when the sisters were planning their next pilgrimage. He waited impatiently, scratching out the days on a makeshift calendar.

Finally, the great day arrived. He took his place by the side of the road. Just as the sun rose, the drawbridge creaked and came down. One by one they crossed it, walking quietly, eyes lowered, single file.

There she was! Her flowing white habit could not conceal her beauty. His heart leapt to his throat. But with one glance at her resolute face, he knew it had all been for naught. He could never sway her from her vows. Crushed and brokenhearted, he turned away.

A familiar high-pitched giggle came floating through the empty hall. Michael had walked LeAnn to her class, and the All-American Golden Girl was saying an extended good-bye to her male counterpart at the door. Just before Sunita walked by, Michael turned around.

She gave him a cool nod, remembering her resolution.

"I really liked your essay, Sunni," he said. She told herself sternly not to notice his dimples.

"Thank you very much," she answered politely. He was standing so close, and he always smelled so nice and clean. "Poverty, chastity, obedience," she muttered under her breath.

"Did you say something?" he asked, leaning closer.

"No—uh, yes," Sunita stammered. "We're extremely late, aren't we?"

But Michael didn't seem to care. He stopped outside the door, cleared his throat, and took a deep breath.

"Listen, Sunni," he blurted out. "Our first tennis match is a week from Monday. Are you going to come cheer me on or not?"

He'd said it so fast that Sunita wasn't sure if she'd heard it. He shifted his weight from one foot to the other and cleared his throat. Michael Morrison was actually nervous. Because of her. Sunita decided that she'd wait on the convent application forms.

"I'll see what I can do, Michael," she said, and smiled, throwing all caution to the wind.

Chapter 7

O n the bus after school, Sunita had a seat all to herself. Michael had tennis practice, LeAnn and Jeannie had cheerleading practice, and Liz had started running track again.

Liz was training seriously this year, trying to beat Bill McTaggart's time in the two-mile. Last year, the two of them had run hard against each other during practice. But at the meets, Bill would stand beside the track during the girls' two-mile race, yelling, "GO, STICK, GO!"

Sunita didn't mind riding the bus alone. She had plenty of important things to think about. What to wear to Traci's party that night. How to remind Dad that he'd promised to drive her to the Graysons' after dinner. And whether Michael would ask her to go to Ziggy's for iced teas after the tennis match.

Girls' tennis started in the spring, and Sunita was hoping to play in the number one spot this year. Her tennis had improved a lot over the summer— and the many times she and Michael had played were part of the reason. Michael was easily the best player on his team. The high school coach had come over last fall to watch him play, even though he'd been only in seventh grade then.

"Think he can skip a grade, Ted?" Sunita had overheard him asking the junior high coach as they watched Michael annihilate his opponent. As the bus traveled on its familiar route, Sunita put on her dark sunglasses and shut her eyes.

Set five in the men's semifinals at Wimbledon. The camera focuses on the face of the defending champ, who wipes the sweat off his forehead with his wristband and frowns.

"Michael Morrison is really giving the champ a run for his money," the announcer tells the television audience.

The camera pans across the crowd, stopping for a second to focus on Princess Diana sitting in the royal box. She claps furiously and yells, "Smashing shot, Michael!"

"Watching all of this is Michael Morrison's beautiful friend, Sunita Sen, who is waiting to play in the women's finals next week."

The camera shifts to Sunita and lingers for a close-up shot. She is sitting back in her box seat and watching quietly, wearing dark glasses and a Ralph Lauren scarf in her hair.

"Hey, you in the back! Hey, kid! Sally—Susie,

whatever your name is!" The bus driver sounded annoyed. "Isn't this your stop?"

Sunita jumped up and swept past the handful of giggling seventh-graders in the front of the bus. She smiled graciously at the bus driver as she climbed out. He was young. One day he would be able to tell his grandkids that the world-famous Sunita Sen had ridden on his route.

The house was quiet. Mom had gone over to the junior college to have coffee with one of her friends, and Didu was taking a nap. Sunita grabbed some cookies and wandered out to the back yard. It was kind of interesting to see the progress her grandfather made each day.

He had completely cleared more than half of the yard of weeds. In one corner, he had piled up a compost heap of leftover food scraps and leaves that he was gradually mixing into the soil. She watched as he pushed the shovel into the ground with his foot and turned over the earth.

"What are you going to plant, Dadu?" she asked.

"Bontu!" he answered, turning around. "What a nice surprise! Just when I was about to venture inside and solicit some advice."

"What kind of advice?"

"I am facing the quintessential gardener's quandary. Shall we plant vegetables exclusively and be completely utilitarian? Or perhaps we should concentrate on aesthetics and plant only flowers? Or shall we attempt a combination of the two?"

Sunita thought for a minute as they looked over the yard together. She handed him a cookie.

"Some vegetables are just as pretty as flowers, don't you think?"

"Ah, yes. A vital point I had overlooked. The ripe red curve of tiny tomatoes, the gleaming orange of a pumpkin against glossy green leaves."

"But Mom does love having fresh flowers in the house."

Her grandfather pushed the shovel into the soil and leaned on it, munching on his cookie.

"A combination it is then," he said. "Vegetables with all of their bounty and flowers in all of their glory. I am planning a trip to the nursery tomorrow morning. Perhaps you and Elizabeth would like to assist me?"

Sunita watched her grandfather's face as he surveyed the yard. He stooped a little, and she was almost as tall as he was. Behind his glasses, she could see dozens of lines that had settled into a comfortable pattern. He looked tired and hot from digging, but his eyes gleamed with anticipation as he imagined blooming flower beds and vines overflowing with ripe vegetables. Maybe he could use some help to carry some of the stuff he needed at the nursery. And who could they possibly run into there?

59

"Sure, Dadu," she answered. "I'm spending the night at the Graysons', remember? But I'll call Liz as soon as she gets back from practice and ask if she wants to join you in the morning."

Her grandfather nodded his thanks and went back to his digging. Sunita hurried upstairs to rummage through her sister's closet, hoping there was something buried underneath all the tie-dyed T-shirts that would be perfect for Traci's party. Her own clothes were all so young.

She was tying a hand-embroidered piece of Kenyan cloth around her white T-shirt dress when her mother came home.

"Does this look okay?" Sunita asked. But Mom didn't answer. She hurried by, clutching a box of tissue. The bedroom door shut firmly behind her.

Sunita stood outside the door. She could hear Mom crying inside and talking to herself, half in Bengali and half in English. She knocked once, softly.

"Mom?" she called. There was no answer, and she knocked again. "It's me, Bontu. Do you want to talk?"

Inside, Mom was quiet.

"No, Bontu. I need to be alone," she called out finally.

Suddenly, Didu popped out of Sunita's old room, her arms outstretched, straining with all her might against an unseen force.

"*My baby!* She needs me!" she cried, giving one mighty tug against whatever was holding her back. She gained some ground, and Sunita could see Dadu holding on to the end of Didu's saree, trying valiantly to keep her in the room. Sunita plastered herself against the wall in case he lost his grip and her grandmother came hurtling down the hall like a big rubber band.

"A grown woman—not your baby anymore," Dadu grunted, digging his heels into the carpet and trying to catch his breath.

Three steps at a time, Sunita's father came running up the stairs, briefcase in hand. Putting one arm around his mother-in-law's shoulder, he steered her firmly away from the bedroom door.

"It's okay, Ma. I'll go in and talk to Ranee."

Sunita went into the kitchen to wait for Geetie's call, wondering what in the world had happened to make Mom so upset. In their bedroom, Dad was listening to Mom and comforting her. In *their* bedroom, Dadu was listening to Didu and comforting her.

Right on cue, the phone rang.

"Did you ever miss a scene around here!" Sunita said, when she heard her sister's voice.

Geetie didn't seem surprised at Mom's strange behavior. "I know why she's upset. One of her colleagues at the college got the promotion Mom should have had."

61

So that was it. Mom's decision to be the perfect Indian daughter was finally demanding a price. "It's her own fault," Sunita said, hardening her heart. "She made the choice to take a year off, and now she's got to live with it."

Geetie sighed. A long, sad sigh that didn't sound anything like her normally enthusiastic self. "We all make choices. Some good, and some bad. Take Maria, for instance. I hope she doesn't have regrets about *her* choices."

"What's wrong with Maria?"

"Oh, nothing. She's just sold her soul, that's all. She's just joined one of those horrible sororities, that's all. And she's a finalist at the cheerleader tryouts. She's forgotten everything we ever learned about beating this male-dominated system. And when I say anything, she just smiles one of those fake, sweet, sorority-girl smiles."

Sunita pictured her sister's friend. Maria had always been pretty and had always had a sweet smile. But she'd never before come out from behind Geetie's powerful shadow.

Geetie sighed again. "Anyway, I have to catch the train. There's an antiplastics rally on campus, but I think I'll skip it and come home for dinner."

Dinner. Sunita glanced at the stove, still gleaming from Mom's vigorous postlunch scrubbing. Obviously, dinner had been overlooked. And the mur-

murs of comfort behind both closed doors sounded as if they would continue for a while.

Happily, Sunita dialed the number of the pizza parlor down the street. She was getting tired of curry day after day. And then, remembering her sister's strange diet, she dialed the number of the take-out vegetarian sushi place.

By the time Mom and Dad finally emerged from their bedroom, Geetie, the pizzas, and the sushi had all arrived. The four Sens sat around the kitchen table, carefully avoiding any discussion about the lost promotion. After a while, they all relaxed. Mom even giggled at one of Dad's silly jokes. With the sushi, the pizza, and just the four of them, it seemed like old times.

Until Didu came shuffling out in her bedroom slippers, hair falling out of its bun, saree rumpled, cheeks streaked with tears.

"My baby!" she wailed, rushing over to Mom.

Sunita's mom sighed. "I'm okay, Ma." she said. "Really."

Mom set her piece of pizza down and stood up. She put her arms around her mother and let her cry. The two of them stayed that way for a long time. Not knowing what else to do, Sunita, Geetie, and Dad concentrated on chewing and stared at their plates.

And then Dadu came in. Rubbing his palms

together, he leaned over the pizza and sniffed rapturously.

"Ahhh! At long last, the delights of pizza await me! Our young friend Elizabeth has been tormenting me with vivid descriptions about this American delicacy. But alas! I was too afraid of insulting our faithful cooks to suggest ordering one."

Didu pulled herself out of Mom's arms to shake her head in disgust.

"Night and day for fifty years, I set his favorite dishes before him, and now he chooses this . . . peet-zuh thing . . . over *my* cooking."

Dadu winked at Sunita and Geetie and put one huge piece on his own plate and another on his wife's plate. After that, they ate with gusto, liberally sprinkling their pizza with the crushed chili peppers the pizza parlor always sent to the Sens' house.

Chapter 8

When Dad dropped Sunita off at the Graysons', he looked so sad that Sunita leaned over and gave him a kiss.

"I'll be back safe and sound in my own bed tomorrow night," she said. "Pick us up in the morning on your way to the nursery with Dadu, okay?"

Sunita was glad Dad hadn't phoned the Graysons ahead of time. She didn't think he'd be thrilled to find out that they were leaving for the weekend. Which was the major reason that Traci was having her party. The overnight visit was traumatic enough for Dad, she thought, waving good-bye as he drove away. Why make it any tougher by sharing insignificant little details?

"Why? Why couldn't I have had a sensible sister like yours?" was Liz's tragic greeting when she opened the door. "My airhead sister has been in the bathroom all evening, while I've been slaving away getting everything ready for her party."

"Geetie's okay, I guess. But she studies all the time, thinks parties are stupid, and hardly ever goes out on a date. How am I supposed to learn anything about the real world from a sister like that?"

Liz handed Sunita the cheese slicer. "I don't know why Traci's even having food," she grumbled. "The kids are only coming to drink the kegs of beer that they heard would be here. I'll have leftover cold cuts in my lunch for weeks."

"I can't believe Traci has the guts to serve beer," said Sunita. Mr. Grayson was the town's assistant chief of police.

"My dad will kill her if he ever finds out," said Liz, brightening up at the thought.

"And he's never going to find out. Right, Elizabeth?" asked Traci, walking into the kitchen. She was wearing a skintight black satin mini and black boots. Her blond hair, so blond that it was almost white, hung shimmering on her bare back.

"You look terrific, Traci," Sunita said.

"Thanks, kid," said Traci, whirling around to give her the full view. "Now you two remember the deal—not a trace of you after ten-thirty."

Liz and Sunita went upstairs to get ready. Sunita loved the bathroom the Grayson girls shared. Two sinks, wall-to-wall carpeting, sunken bathtub, vanity mirror, cushioned chair, and bright lights. Sunita sat down in front of the vanity mirror and gazed at herself glumly.

"I'll never look as glamorous as your sister. Especially with Dad's ridiculous hang-up over makeup."

Her eyes swept across the countertop. Creamy pink and crimson tubes of lipstick, sparkling earrings and glittery necklaces, rainbow palettes of eye shadow, and delicate glass vials of perfume samples were strewn together in a tantalizing jumble.

She reached for some bright red lipstick, put it on, and blew a kiss at herself. Out of the corner of her eye, she noticed Liz holding a pair of dangling earrings to her ears.

Sunita spun around. "Liz, those look great! You definitely should get your ears pierced."

Liz put the earrings down quickly. "I don't know. It seems kind of silly to punch holes in your ears."

"Thank goodness Indian girls get their ears pierced when they're babies. Wearing earrings is the one battle I haven't had to fight."

Sunita watched as her friend studied herself in the mirror. Liz's usual two minutes in front of a mirror were during her morning routine, when she splashed her face with water and ran a comb through her hair before hurrying downstairs for breakfast. Diplomacy wins the day, Sunita reminded herself.

Carefully, casually, she said, "You might try that light-colored tube of lipstick over there and see how it looks."

Liz looked over suspiciously, but Sunita was humming to herself and concentrating on curling her eyelashes.

After a long silence, the girls turned to each other at exactly the same moment. "How do I look?" they asked in unison, and then burst out laughing.

"You look about forty-two years old," said Liz.

"I guess it takes a little practice," admitted Sunita, wiping a huge clump of lipstick off her front tooth.

The party turned out to be a disappointment. Traci had instructed the girls to sit by the stereo system and play the compact disks she had stacked. So this is what you do at a high school party, Sunita thought. Stand around, laugh a lot, and drink one beer after another. Guys look at girls and girls pretend not to look at guys. Until they start making out, which Traci and one of her admirers had been doing continuously on the couch.

"Pass the chips," Liz screamed once over the music.

"What?" Sunita screamed back.

Liz tried turning the volume down, but Traci interrupted her make-out session, stormed over, and turned it up again.

Yawning, the girls went upstairs at ten to watch a video in the Graysons' bedroom.

"My ears are still ringing from last night," said Liz the next morning, shaking out her arms and brushing the dirt off her T-shirt.

The girls were in the Sens' back yard. They had just brought in the last bags of fertilizer from the car. Packs of seeds, cuttings, and cartons of bulbs were everywhere. Dadu was already measuring out a flower bed in one corner of the yard.

"From the music or from your dad yelling at Traci?" asked Sunita. The Graysons had surprised everyone by coming home. When Mr. Grayson tripped over a beer keg on his way in from the garage, the party had ended abruptly.

"I think she's grounded for life," said Liz. She wandered over to a patch of sunshine in a grassy corner of the yard and lay down, stretching out like a cat. Sunita joined her.

"It's so peaceful back here. I don't know why you don't just give in and do your science experiment out here," Liz said.

Liz was right. It was a peaceful place. "Maybe I will," answered Sunita. "What are you doing for yours?"

"I've got a great one. You know how I'm always

69

biting my nails, right? And how my mom's always bugging me to stop?"

Sunita nodded and rolled her eyes. It was one of the most predictable exchanges in the Grayson home.

Liz grinned. "I've got a great plan to help Mom break her bad habit of nagging me. I'm coating three of my most bitten fingernails with different disgusting substances to test which one will help me stop biting."

She held up her index finger. "This fourth nail will be my control group with nothing on it. But get this—Mom can't say anything to me during the entire experiment, because if she bugs me just when I'm about to bite nail number two, it'll have an unfair advantage over the other three nails."

"Your mom'll see right through you. She always does."

"I know," Liz said, sighing. "But it's worth a try. Anyway, maybe Dadu has an idea for yours. Mind if I ask him?"

Sunita shrugged. "Go ahead," she said.

Liz walked over to where Dadu stood scribbling measurements on a piece of scratch paper. Sunita followed, pretending to be interested in a butterfly that was hovering nearby.

Dadu didn't notice them. He was muttering to himself, adding and subtracting figures furiously. "Crocuses for autumn and others for spring. Tulips

70

one foot apart. A necklace of golden daffodils. And irises. Ahh! Yes, we will weave a thread of purple in with the gold . . ."

Liz planted herself in front of him. "Dadu, we need your advice about something."

Dadu looked at her over his glasses. "Yes, Elizabeth?"

After she explained the experiment to him, she waited. So did Sunita. Dadu was quiet for a minute or so, and then began quoting softly. " 'A sower went out to sow his seed. And as he sowed, some fell by the wayside—' "

"Hey, wait a minute!" interrupted Liz. "That's not from an Indian book. That's from the Bible!"

Sunita's grandfather frowned. "Such words of great wisdom can never belong only to one people," he said, his voice sounding almost severe. Liz and Sunita exchanged looks, surprised at his tone.

After a short pause, his voice regained its usual gentle singsong rhythm. "Will you paraphrase the rest of the story for us, Elizabeth?"

"I studied it in Sunday school ages ago. I think it's got something to do with different kinds of soil, and how only one of them is good."

"That's right. Every true gardener knows how important the quality of soil is to the eventual harvest. Bontu, I recommend that you try four different types of soil—some trodden, some rocky, some thorny, and finally some good, rich soil. Now, if you young ladies will excuse me, I must return to my calculations."

Liz had planned to jog home from the Sens' house, and she began her stretching routine. Sunita walked around the yard thoughtfully. The part that Dadu had turned up and mixed in with the compost looked dark and rich. The soil around the lawn furniture was hard and packed from lots of footsteps. Another area was rocky, and another looked weedy and thorny.

"Well?" asked Liz.

"I guess it's not the worst idea I've heard," answered Sunita.

After Liz left, Sunita grabbed a trowel and began to dig a shallow hole near the lawn furniture. Dadu was squatting in the far end of the garden working more of the compost into the soil. She hummed under her breath as she dug holes and scattered forget-me-not seeds.

Chapter 9

"Do you think fish, chicken, cauliflower, eggplant, lentils, and rice will be enough food?" asked Didu doubtfully a week later, on Sunday afternoon. An Indian family was visiting that evening, and she and Mom had been cooking in the kitchen all day.

Sunita was peeling potatoes. She groaned to herself. Another exciting night watching *Return of the Killer Squids* or some other classic favorite of the Banerjee brats. And still more brilliant conversation with Ravi.

Ravi was the Banerjees' oldest son. Like Sunita, he was in the eighth grade. He went to another school, but he and Sunita had hung out together at all the Indian parties and gatherings since they were little kids. When their parents visited each other, they'd ride bikes together or talk or listen to music.

But last year, Ravi had changed. When he saw Sunita, he ducked his head and blushed. When she asked him a question, he stuttered and stammered and hid behind the hair that hung over his glasses. His voice had changed, and it tended to squeak when he got nervous. Sunita would feel herself getting nervous for him, and then she would start to stutter and stammer. Being together had become excruciating for both of them. These days, Ravi usually brought a book along when his family visited. He and Sunita would read while his little brothers tore the house apart.

The evening started out predictably. Ravi stumbled into the house and awkwardly gave Didu and Dadu *pronam*—touching first their feet and then his own forehead and heart in the sign of respect Bengali young people were required to give to their elders. Mrs. Banerjee, looking sleek in silk pants and an angora sweater embroidered with pearls, bent down to give Dadu and Didu *pronam*.

Sunita thought she looked out of place giving *pronam*. Ravi's mom was one of the leading doctors in Berkeley and always seemed elegantly put together. Dadu and Didu didn't seem to care. They smiled and touched her head, giving her the blessing elder people gave to younger people.

The Banerjee boys roared into the house, ignoring all the older people and clutching an assortment of video games and movies. Sunita and Ravi followed them silently downstairs. Ravi hunched over his book, his hair hiding his face from Sunita. After twenty minutes of listening to the twins argue as they watched a loud Kung Fu–type movie, Sunita felt like doing something drastic.

A swoon? Nobody would notice. A graceful, sweeping exit? Mom would kill her if she hid out in Geetie's room all night. Rush over to Ravi, toss his book on the floor, and throw herself on his lap? Sunita pictured herself flinging back Ravi's hair to gaze deeply into his eyes. He'd be the youngest person ever to die of a coronary.

Just as she was feeling ready to risk Mom's wrath and escape upstairs, Dadu walked down the stairs. He walked over to the television, watched for a minute, and then turned it off. The twins groaned, temporarily united in their loss.

"The inventor of television would surely regret such abuse of his creation," Dadu said. "Shall we try something that challenges our acumen slightly more?"

He walked over to the games closet and pulled out the Carom board he'd brought from Calcutta. Sunita's parents had been delighted to see it. They had reminisced about the hours they used to spend playing Carom with their friends when they were young.

The board was about the size of a card table. Dadu put it on the floor. Sunita, Ravi, and the twins watched as he sprinkled talcum powder on it and carefully arranged the pieces in the center of the board.

"The powder makes the pieces slide faster," he explained. "Ravi, you and Sunita try to knock the black pieces into these four corner holes. The twins and I will take the white pieces. The first team to knock all their pieces into the holes wins."

Sunita sighed, and Ravi reluctantly closed his book. Any game with the twins was bound to result in chaos, but neither of them could disobey the note of authority in Dadu's voice. Sitting cross-legged on the floor on opposite sides of the board, they listened as he explained the rest of the rules.

"Keep your elbows off the board. Place this larger piece on the black stripe in front of you. Use the larger piece to knock the smaller pieces into the corners. To hit the larger piece, put your forefinger and thumb together, like this, and flick your forefinger against the larger piece."

A twin tried to imitate him and missed completely.

"It's a lot like pool!" said Ravi. His voice squeaked, and the twins giggled and elbowed each other.

Dadu ignored them. "It is a lot like pool, but without the cues—the cues are replaced by our fingers. Let us begin, shall we?"

They began to get the hang of it after a few tries.

When Mom called them to dinner, the competition had become fierce. The twins were adequate, Sunita and Ravi had improved rapidly, and Dadu was awesome. His fingers flicked with deadly accuracy, and two or three white pieces shot into the corners each time.

"We're almost done!" Sunita yelled, when Mom called again.

She frowned in concentration. There were two black pieces and only one white piece left on the board. There was a slim chance of hitting both black pieces in with one shot. Fingering the larger piece, she looked up at Ravi, wondering if she should ask him what to do.

"Go for it, Bontu!" he said, grinning. It was the first time he'd called her by name in a year, and Sunita almost dropped the piece in surprise.

She missed her shot, and the twins yelled at the top of their lungs when one of them made the winning shot. Sunita and Ravi walked side by side to the dinner table, arguing over whether or not she'd chosen the right shot to try. Their mothers looked at each other and raised their eyebrows. Sunita's mom glanced at Dadu suspiciously, but he was busy teasing the twins about how much food they were heaping on their plates.

Chapter 10

All weekend long, Sunita imagined what might happen on Monday at the tennis match.

"I can hardly wait," she told Liz on the phone.

"You'll probably sit in the bleachers next to Michael's mom," Liz said, getting excited for her friend. "He's bound to play awesome tennis with you cheering him on."

"I wonder if we'll go to Ziggy's after the match," Sunita said. She pictured herself face to face with Michael in one of the private corner booths. "Maybe then I can take your advice and tell him the truth about why he can't come over. A wonderful guy like Michael Morrison wouldn't hold my weird family against me, right?"

"Right. Call me the moment you get back from Ziggy's."

After her last class on Monday, Sunita hurried to the bathroom to brush her hair. Ilana Taylor was standing in front of the mirror, applying lipstick. Her hair was woven into dozens of delicately beaded braids. With every movement, the sapphire blue beads clinked together, sounding like tiny wind chimes. Ilana's eyes caught Sunita's watching in the mirror.

"You always look so elegant, Ilana," Sunita blurted out.

Ilana raised her eyebrows slightly, but the rest of her face stayed composed.

"Modeling school for three years," she explained matter-of-factly. And then she studied Sunita's reflection in the mirror, almost as though she were appraising a piece of art.

Sunita straightened up self-consciously. She was wearing an oversized pink sweater over blue jeans— an outfit she'd selected after trying on almost everything in her closet. There was a big pile of clothes on her bed that she'd have to deal with later.

"You really don't need too much makeup," Ilana said finally. She rummaged in her purse and pulled out a tube of rose-colored lipstick. "Here. Put a little of this on."

Sunita carefully applied the lipstick, making sure none got on her teeth.

"With your skin tone, you have to be careful with

makeup," Ilana said. She hesitated and readjusted her scarf. "Would you like me to show you how sometime?"

Ilana's voice was light, but Sunita could sense her waiting for a reply. The Taylor family had moved into the neighborhood a year ago, and Ilana had kept to herself all through the seventh grade. This was the first time that she had made any effort at a friendship with Sunita. Or with anybody else, as far as Sunita knew.

"That would be great, Ilana," she said. And then something in Ilana's face made her say impulsively, "Hey, what are you doing now? Come help me cheer Michael on at the tennis match."

When Ilana smiled, Sunita realized it was the first time that she'd seen a real smile on the other girl's face. Her "modeling smile" used the lips only, and didn't make her eyes sparkle as they did now.

"I'll join you for a little while," Ilana said. "My mom's coming to pick me up in half an hour."

They headed out of the girls' room and walked down the hall, side by side. Suddenly, from somewhere behind them, they heard a loud whisper. "Check it out—the colored girls stick together."

Both girls kept walking, but each knew the other had heard. They passed a phone booth, and Sunita stopped beside it, fumbling in her purse for change.

"Uh—I just remembered I need to make an urgent phone call, Ilana," she said. "You go on. I'll be there in just a bit."

Ilana stopped too. "Do you want me to wait, Sunni?" she asked. Her voice was calm, as though nothing had changed.

"No thanks," Sunita mumbled. "This may take a while."

She looked up and saw the other girl's eyes fill with scorn. Giving Sunita a perfect modeling smile— lips only, no eyes—Ilana walked away.

By the time Sunita got to the courts, the bleachers were almost full. Ilana was nowhere in sight, and Sunita was ashamed at how relieved she felt. She shaded her eyes against the sun, looking for an empty seat. The high school coach and a group of his players, their heads pivoting back and forth, were watching Michael and his opponent warm up. She could see Liz and Bill McTaggart in the distance, two tiny figures on the track beyond the bleachers, their long legs hitting the ground side by side in an easy rhythm.

"Yoo-hoo! Over here, Sunni!" called a voice. A familiar voice. Sunita swallowed. It was LeAnn, sitting right next to Mrs. Morrison. The more groupies to cheer the tennis star on the better, she thought grimly. Michael's mom waved and patted an empty space on her other side.

"Aren't you dying in that sweater, Sunni?" asked LeAnn, as Sunita sat down. The cheerleaders' workout clothes were clingy nylon bike pants and cropped T-shirts, tailor-made to show off LeAnn's curves and long, slim legs. Legs that were shaved, of course. LeAnn's personal hygiene was not subject to Geetie's strict political standards.

Sunita glanced down. Suddenly, her jean-clad legs looked like two short stumps holding up a big pink barrel. And LeAnn was right—the afternoon sunshine was hot. Sunita felt beads of perspiration begin to roll down her neck.

LeAnn was chattering on. "Can you believe that the high school coach brought half his team to watch? Michael told me all about his strategy last night."

So Michael and LeAnn had been together on Sunday night. Suddenly, spending the evening with Ravi Banerjee playing Carom seemed childish and boring.

LeAnn turned to Mrs. Morrison. "There's just no hope for the other guy, is there, Kate?"

"It should be a good match," answered Mrs. Morrison. She turned to Sunita. "I've missed your visits, Sunita. How have you been?"

"Oh, busy with school and stuff," answered

Sunita. "In fact, I can only stay for a little while today. I've got tons of homework."

"Oh, Sunni, lighten up," said LeAnn. "You'll get straight A's like you always do. You should have heard Mr. Riley rave about Sunni's essay, Kate."

"Michael told me about it," said Mrs. Morrison. "But I'd love to hear more."

"Morrison to serve," someone announced. Sunita breathed a sigh of relief as Michael's mother's attention shifted to the court. She certainly didn't intend to drag the details of her grandparents' romance in front of anyone ever again. Especially Mrs. Morrison.

One day, when Michael had gone to help his mom bring in groceries, Sunita was alone in the Morrisons' family room. She had reached for his parents' wedding album. She'd caught her breath at the beauty of the first photo.

Standing in front of a stained glass window, Mrs. Morrison was lifting her face to receive Mr. Morrison's kiss. The white lace of her dress and veil spilled across the floor and over his shiny black shoes. When Michael and his mom came in, Sunita had hurriedly shut the album. She'd felt like an uninvited guest barging into a sacred ceremony.

"Kate, Mom told me some members of the club wanted to build clay tennis courts! Aren't you glad they ended up voting against it?" LeAnn chirped.

It was "Kate" this and "Kate" that until Sunita could have screamed. Michael won the first set 6–3. LeAnn clapped and squealed each time he won a point, keeping up a constant stream of chatter in between. When the score was Morrison 4, Roberts 0 in the second set, Sunita stood up to leave.

"Off to study again?" asked LeAnn. "We're going to Ziggy's after the match, so Michael and I won't get anything done as usual."

So Michael was going to Ziggy's after the match. To gaze into LeAnn's blue eyes and discover another hundred things they had in common. Sunita's daydream crashed so loudly inside her head that she thought everybody else would jump.

"Good-bye, Mrs. Morrison," Sunita said. She couldn't bring herself to say good-bye to LeAnn.

"It was good to see you again, Sunita," said Michael's mom. Her voice was kind, as though she could see right through Sunita's forced politeness to the misery inside.

"Bye, Sunni," called LeAnn, as Sunita turned and fled.

She didn't even cry when she was safely in Geetie's room. She was too angry. She tossed all the clothes she'd tried on that morning on the floor, calling herself all kinds of names. Idiot. Moron. Fool. Jerk.

How could she ever have imagined that someone like Michael Morrison could ever understand her dilemma? People like the Morrisons and Schaeffers were made of apple pie and country clubs and stained glass windows and pot roast. The Sens were made of chicken curry and sarees and sitar music and incense. Michael was even a Boy Scout, for heaven's sake.

She would leave the all-American types to each other from now on, she decided, tossing her pink sweater onto the pile of dirty clothes. She had been crazy even to consider Liz's advice. In fact, she'd call up Aunty Liz and tell her just how wrong she had been.

Liz answered the phone. "For the tenth time, Jason, Traci's not home," she said, sounding exasperated.

"It's me, Liz," said Sunni.

"Oh, sorry. What happened? How come you're home so early? When I left, it looked like the match was still going."

Sunita painted a description of the match in a few graphic words.

"He invited both of you to the match? I don't get it."

"Why not? He wouldn't want anybody to think I was his girlfriend, would he? With her blond hair, blue eyes, and perfect body, LeAnn probably scored big points for Michael with those high school guys."

"Why did he ask you to go, then?"

"I don't know. Maybe he likes having two girls fighting over him. Or else he probably feels sorry for me."

"Oh, Sunni. You're the only one who feels sorry for you. Everyone else thinks you're cute and smart and fun to be with."

"Until they find out about my bizarre family. Is there any other home in America today where boys are not allowed to come over? Where a girl practically has to beg to spend the night at her best friend's house? Where people eat with their hands and wear sheets in public?"

"I love your family, Sunita Sen."

"But you're—you, Liz. You've known us forever. Let's face it. I'm stuck in my weird family, and Michael's stuck in his normal family. And there is nothing we can do about it. Anyway," Sunita said, "I've got to go. Mom and Dad are out on their walk, and I want to grab a bite to eat before they get back."

As soon as she hung up, the phone rang. She picked it up, expecting to hear her sister's voice.

"Hi, Geetie," she said glumly.

"Sunni?" asked a voice that definitely wasn't her sister's. It was Michael.

"This is Sunita," she answered after a long pause. "Who is this?"

"It's me, Michael."

"Yes?"

"I won the second set six—love." She knew he was waiting for her to say something about the match, but she was quiet.

"Are you feeling okay, Sunni? You left early, and Mom said you seemed a bit tired or something."

She steeled her heart against the concern in his voice. "I'm fine," she said. "I left because you seemed to have enough fans there."

"What are you talking about? You know my mom always comes to my matches. Oh . . . and LeAnn came. Her mom and mine were sorority sisters in college. We've known each other since we were born."

Sunita took a deep breath and made her voice sound crisp, the way her dad's secretary sounded on the phone. "You and LeAnn are so much alike, Michael. You and I . . . We don't really have too much in common, do we?"

It was his turn to be quiet. "What do you mean, Sunni?" he asked finally.

"I mean what I said. Let's just leave it at that, okay?"

She sensed his anger even before he spoke. "I guess I will leave it at that," he said. And then he hung up.

Sunita replaced the receiver slowly, feeling cold and detached—as if she'd become the person she'd been pretending to be on the phone. She could hear her grandmother coming into the kitchen. Grabbing her observation notebook, she slipped downstairs and went outside.

Dadu was using every bit of daylight to plant the bulbs before the first frost. The yard was starting to look orderly after hours of his patient weeding, fertilizing, watering, and planting. A few crocus shoots were poking up already. He was always careful to leave untouched the areas she was using for her experiment.

She walked over to the packed soil around the lawn furniture where she'd planted the first group of seeds. Nothing. There were no signs of life there at all, even though Sunita watered all four places evenly. She wrote the date and the four types of soil on a clean page in her notebook: *Packed, Rocky, Weedy, Rich.*

In the rocky soil, some thin, frail-looking plants were trying their best to squeeze through the pebbles. She couldn't tell if any flowers were beginning to grow underneath the thick weeds. But in the dark, rich soil by the compost heap, tiny green shoots were already springing up.

Her grandfather came to stand beside her. "How is your experiment progressing, my granddaughter?" her grandfather asked.

"Predictably. It's turning out to be a boring experiment, actually."

"Most scientific experiments are predictable, and

admittedly, a bit boring. Put certain elements to-gether, wait for a while, and eventually see the out-come you expected to see. The most exciting experiments are the unpredictable ones."

"I don't know," said Sunita. "Predictable experi-ments may be boring. But there's something com-fortable about them." She was quiet for a minute, thinking about what she'd said. Dadu waited.

"Sometimes . . . Sometimes I wish things in my life were more predictable," she said finally. "But they're not. I'm like a wild new experiment. Like somebody's taken a few elements that are Indian and a few that are American and some that are just me, Sunita Sen. And they've mixed them all to-gether and are waiting to see what in the world will come out."

"I suppose you children are an experiment, Bontu. But your grandmother and I have been ob-serving the experiment with great satisfaction. And fascination, if I might add."

Sunita sighed. "I wish Mom and Dad had stayed in India. Then I would be one hundred percent Indian, like those cousins Didu is always bragging about. Or if I had been born here and had been American—I mean really American—you know, born-in-the-U.S.A. and all that patriotic land-where-my-fathers-died stuff. Maybe then life would be less complicated."

"Less complicated, maybe. More predictable,

maybe. But never, never as fearfully and wonderfully woven together as the life of my beautiful granddaughter Sunita Sen."

Sunita giggled. For the first time in what seemed like ages. "You're not biased at all, are you?" she asked her grandfather.

Chapter 11

A huge pile of raincoats lay abandoned by the door of the cafeteria. Distracted teachers tried to stop food fights. Kids groaned when Mr. Riley intercepted the flattened milk carton they were tossing across the room. Sunita and Liz sat squashed at a crowded table that was out of the line of fire.

Liz was drawing ovals on a paper napkin and explaining her strategy for the afternoon track meet. Every now and then she munched on the sandwich Sunita's mom had made from leftover chicken curry. Sunita tore Liz's peanut-butter-and-jelly sandwich into little squares, nodding her head once in a while and making listening noises.

In one corner of the cafeteria, LeAnn, Jeannie, and a bunch of other kids were laughing and talking. Michael was with them, but he was deep in a discussion with one of the guys. About tennis, I bet,

Sunita thought to herself. Sure enough, Michael bent his elbow and straightened it, flicking his wrist at the end.

Sunita had spent the whole week avoiding Michael, trying not to notice that he was avoiding her just as carefully. She had hurried through the halls with her head down and had been the first one on the bus after school. And she hated the pang of guilt she felt when she saw Ilana Taylor's slender, graceful figure—reserved, aloof, always slightly apart from the rest of the students.

Michael, Ilana . . . There weren't too many of her classmates she felt comfortable with these days. Not since that awful day of the tennis match, when she and Ilana had overheard that voice whispering behind them. It could have belonged to any one of Sunita's classmates, and she was determined to discover which one. Like a police dog on the hunt for a criminal's scent, she listened intently whenever anybody whispered in class.

Now, her eyes went back to the crowd in the corner. LeAnn looked irritated. Michael was still discussing tennis. Bill McTaggart and John Rostowski were playing catch with a tube of lipstick. Jeannie was squealing, running back and forth trying to grab it.

Suddenly, Sunita felt as if she was watching them from miles away.

Alone in her bungalow, she wanders over to the telescope that looks out over the sea. A big luxury ocean liner appears on the horizon. Squinting through the lens, she can make out a blond woman holding a champagne glass, surrounded by admiring men wearing tuxedoes.

Idly she wonders who they are and where they are heading. Then she squares her shoulders and turns back to the novel she has been writing in isolation for three years—a sequel to an earlier best-seller—

"Sunita, can I ask you something?" Liz's voice sounded anxious, and Sunita turned to her friend.

"Of course. What is it?"

Liz looked uncomfortable. "Well, last year, we'd go to Ziggy's after every meet, just the two of us," she mumbled. "I explained that to Bill, and told him I had to ask you before he could join us this afternoon."

Sunita made herself smile. The last thing she wanted to do was spend the afternoon with one of LeAnn's admirers—Bill McTaggart. "Did I forget to tell you? I can't make it to the meet today. I'll hear all about it this weekend, okay?"

"But you always come to my meets and cheer me on," Liz said. She stared at the peanut-butter-and-jelly squares Sunita had arranged on her plate. "Bill's a lot of fun when you get to know him, Sunni. He's not really even like a guy at all. I mean—he even likes those old Monty Python flicks I'm always trying to get you to see." She paused again. "His brother's taking us to a Monty Python marathon in Berkeley next week."

It took Sunita a few seconds to realize what Liz was saying. Bill McTaggart was not a member of LeAnn Schaeffer's fan club. Bill McTaggart—lanky Bill McTaggart with his oversized glasses, oversized T-shirts, and oversized unlaced tennis shoes—was the lone male member in Elizabeth Grayson's fan club. And Liz was actually going out on sort of a date with him.

Sunita was surprised at how hurt she felt. I always thought I'd be the first one to have a real date, she thought. The new aloof, detached Sunita took over, making Sunita get up.

"Sorry, I can't make it," she said coldly. "Good luck at your meet." She gathered her things and strode away.

But as she emptied her tray, she couldn't help looking back. Liz was staring gloomily into the distance, long legs sticking out under the table as she twirled one curl around her finger.

She comes running across the schoolyard, red curls and green ribbons bouncing on her head. "Will you be my partner?" she asks, holding out her hand. And Sunita is swept into the hilarity of a three-legged race on her first day of school in a strange town.

Slowly, Sunita turned around and walked back to the table.

"Liz, you nut," she said, sitting down. "Why didn't you tell me that you liked Bill?"

Liz's face lit up. Then she groaned. "Oh, Sunni! I don't even know if I *like him* like him. I mean I like him, I've always liked him, but . . ."

Sunita grinned. "I get it," she said. Bill Mc-Taggart—Liz's first swain. She turned to appraise him with new eyes. Maybe he was the missing link in Sunita's plan to bring her best friend into normal adolescence.

He was the missing link, all right. He was standing on his head on top of a battered folding chair that was precariously balanced on top of the table. Both arms were outstretched, and Jeannie's lipstick was clenched between his teeth. Every now and then, he looked over at Liz to see if she was watching.

She turned back to her friend, who was doing a poor job of pretending not to watch.

"He's so unique, isn't he, Sunni?" Liz said, popping peanut-butter-and-jelly squares into her mouth one by one.

Sunita shrugged. Liz was happy, and that was all that counted.

"He certainly is, Liz," she answered. "Listen, you and Bill have fun at Ziggy's after the meet. You'll probably get rained out anyway. And I want to hear all about the juicy details when you get home, okay?"

Liz's green eyes gazed earnestly from behind her round glasses at Sunita.

"Are you sure you don't want to come to the meet? I'm worried about you, Sunni. You've been moping around ever since the Tennis Match Disaster."

"I am not moping around," Sunita snapped. "I am moving on with my life."

"Calm down, calm down," Liz said. She pulled her glasses down to the tip of her nose and peered over them at Sunita. "You young whippersnappers always get riled up so easy."

Sunita had to grin. Liz did an amazing imitation of a crotchety little old lady. It always gave Sunita a foretaste of what life would be like in six decades or so, when both of them would really be little old ladies. But knowing Liz, by then she would be doing an amazing imitation of a nerdy little teenager.

Chapter 12

When Sunita got home that afternoon, she found a note on the kitchen table. "Bontu," it said, "gone to meet Dad in the city. Leftover curry in fridge for dinner. Love, Mom, Didu, and Dadu."

It was strangely quiet in the house. The mail had arrived, and she flipped through it idly. A huge red envelope in the shape of a heart caught her eye. Big block letters across the front announced, "Mrs. Ria Majumdar—You and Your Date Can Win a Free Weekend in New York City!" The return address said, "The *Endless Hope* Plot Solution Contest, Star Television Studios, New York, New York." Sunita grinned as she put the envelope on her grandmother's pillow.

She wandered out into the back yard. The sky had cleared up after lunch, but new storm clouds were gathering over the hills. The wind rattled the trees, shaking down a layer of golden leaves over Dadu's flower beds. Sunita shivered and turned back inside as drops of rain began to fall again. She watched until it became a steady downpour and then dialed Liz's number.

"Mrs. Grayson? I guess the track meet must have been canceled by now. Is Liz home yet?"

"Sorry, Sunni. Liz just called. Get this. Both teams were all geared up to compete, so they decided to find a way to battle it out indoors. At this very moment, they are locked in mortal combat—at the bowling alley! I'm leaving right now to go shopping, and I'm supposed to pick her up in a couple of hours."

After turning down Mrs. Grayson's offer to drop her off at the bowling alley, Sunita sat down and finished her homework. Sunita Sen, social flop. The only teenager in America with nothing better to do on a Friday afternoon than her homework. She slammed her notebook shut, realizing that she hadn't watched *Casablanca* in a long time.

Sam, the black piano player, was pouring his heart into their favorite song. Sunita sat back, ready to lose herself in one of her favorite scenes.

But she just couldn't seem to get into it. All kinds of questions she'd never asked before kept popping into her head. Didn't Sam have a life of his own? Why did he have to call her Miss Ilsa when she just called him Sam? Where was Casablanca anyway?

Wasn't it in Africa? Why were there no black Africans in the entire movie? And why was she starting to sound like Mr. Riley?

Mr. Riley had spent the past week asking them to identify cultural and racial stereotypes in popular movies. The class had enjoyed watching current videos and discussing them. They were going to look at some classic children's books next week.

Sunita turned off the movie and headed upstairs with a determined look in her eye.

When Geetie came home, Sunita was curled up on the couch under an afghan, frowning over a battered old copy of *The Secret Garden*.

Sunita followed her sister into the kitchen. "This used to be my favorite book in the whole world," she announced.

"Isn't it still?" Geetie asked, peering into the fridge past the chicken curry. "When is Mom going to get it through her head that I'm a vegetarian?" she grumbled.

"Listen to this." Sunita began to read.

"It's different in India," said Mistress Mary disdainfully. She could scarcely stand this.

But Martha was not at all crushed.

"Eh! I can see it's different," she answered almost sympathetically. "I dare say it's because there's such a lot o' blacks there instead o' respectable white people.

99

*When I heard you was comin' from India I thought
you was a black too."*

Mary sat up in bed furious.

*"What!" she said. "What! You thought I was a
native. You—you daughter of a pig!"*

She slapped the book shut. "Can you believe that?"
she demanded.

Geetie's voice came out of the depths of the fridge
where she was foraging for tofu. "Don't get disillusioned, kid. Frances Burnett was a product of her
time. India was under British rule for years, you
know. You can still appreciate the story."

"I guess so. It just makes me mad that I never
noticed all this stuff before!"

Something in Sunita's voice made Geetie pull her
head out of the fridge. Sunita braced herself for a
lecture. Instead, her sister put one hand lightly
against Sunita's cheek.

"Welcome to the real world, Bontu," she said
softly.

Chapter 13

"Will somebody please explain why such horrible orange faces glare at me from every store window?" asked Didu. She was hovering over her son-in-law's plate, ready to fill it with more rice the moment he emptied it. During their first or second meal in America, she'd scolded her daughter when Sunita's dad had reached for seconds on chicken curry. "For shame, Ranee," she'd said. "You've forgotten that a good Indian woman fills her family members' plates *before* they have to ask."

Mom was lying on the sofa in the dark living room. Like some kind of invalid, thought Sunita.

"Those orange faces are pumpkins, Mother," Sunita's mom called out when nobody answered Didu's question. "They are decorations to celebrate Halloween this weekend. Bontu, why don't you explain to Didu and Dadu what Halloween is?"

Lately, Sunita sat silently through meals, eating as fast as she could. "Can't you even make a tiny effort at conversation?" Mom had pleaded, coming into Geetie's room for a private conference with her younger daughter. "You just stare down at your plate and shovel in your food, like—like it's medicine or something. It's very unnerving."

"Sunita, did you hear me?" Mom asked now. Her voice had an edge to it.

"I don't really know," Sunita answered shortly, realizing that she was telling the truth. She had no idea what Halloween was all about, even though she'd spent every year since the first grade carefully choosing a costume. Last year, after coming home and seeing just one or two other kids their age on the street, she and Liz had realized that it was their last stint as trick-or-treaters.

"I know what Halloween is," said her dad, pushing away his plate with a sigh. "It's a day when kids have complete license to litter my lawn with all kinds of candy wrappers and overturn my garbage cans."

Didu looked confused. "Have some more rice, Arun," she said, her tone of voice implying that her son-in-law was too dazed with hunger to make much sense.

"Which reminds me, Bontu," continued Sunita's father, "where is the Halloween party this year?"

Each year, one of the families in the neighborhood hosted a Halloween party and scavenger hunt.

Kids of all sizes split up into teams and dispersed, lists in hand, hunting for all kinds of strange items. From the beginning, their parents had insisted on two rules: every kid in the neighborhood had to be invited to the party, and they could only scavenge at houses where people whom they knew lived.

Sunita was dreading Halloween. The party was going to be at Jeannie Adams's house. She pictured LeAnn and her crowd ringing the doorbell, Dadu opening it, his eyes gleaming with pleasure, and Didu offering them food, her heavy accent impossible to understand. She thought of LeAnn and Jeannie giggling and rolling their eyes at each other.

"The Adamses are hosting it, Dad," answered Sunita. "I'm not going this year." If only she could make her family disappear on Halloween.

"Why not?" asked her father. "Last year you and Liz had your costumes for the party all planned out even before school started."

"I'm not feeling into Halloween this year. And Liz is probably doing something with Bill Mc-Taggart, anyway." She turned to her grandmother, deliberately changing the subject. "Didu, are you really planning on entering that soap opera contest?"

Her dad gave his daughter a sharp glance. The whole family knew that Didu had been spending hours closeted in Sunita's old room, working on the perfect plot solution for the *Endless Hope* contest. She filled the wastepaper basket every day with crumpled sheets of paper. She kept the whole family up by pecking on Dad's ancient typewriter late into the night.

Dad's theory was that the original writer of the show's complicated plot had entered an insane asylum before finishing the plot, and the producers were hoping to discover another mind like his among the show's dedicated viewers. Or else the whole thing was a bogus promotion that nobody would ever win. Of course he didn't tell Didu any of his theories.

"Your grandmother not only plans to enter that contest, Bontu," he said now. "She plans to win that trip to New York City. And if she does, I'm sure I can get some time off to escort her."

"No, no, Arun. You won't go with me," Didu told him. "Ever since we were first married, your father-in-law has talked of visiting the Large Apple—New York City. We shall go together."

"Well, if for some crazy reason you don't win, I'm sure we can arrange a trip to the East Coast for two," Dad said. "But you haven't really seen California yet—which gives me a tremendous idea of how to spend Halloween weekend."

Sunita hadn't been paying attention, but when she heard Halloween mentioned, she looked up.

"I hope this year the little goblins will be happy with a bag of candy taped to the door," her dad continued, watching Sunita's face.

"Why?" called Sunita's mom from the other room. "Aren't we going to answer the door?"

"It just struck me that Halloween is the perfect time to visit Yosemite National Park. Get it? Everybody else is at home doing their normal, boring Halloween routine, and we'll have the gorgeous Yosemite valley all to ourselves."

Sunita's face lit up. "That's a terrific idea, Dad! Didu and Dadu will love Yosemite!" Ignoring her father's imitation heart attack, she jumped up and threw her arms around him.

Her mom came into the dining room, looking happier than Sunita had seen her look in a long time. "That is a great idea," she said, smiling at her husband.

The next day, Jeannie Adams walked over to Sunita before social studies started. "Are you coming to the party or not, Sunni?" she asked.

"We'll be gone this weekend," Sunita answered. "But we're leaving candy on the door."

"Gone? On Halloween?" asked Jeannie. "I thought only the neighborhood grinches did the candy-on-the-door thing."

"Looks like the Sinister Sen family is asking for tricks this year," said John Rostowski, grinning. He had teased Sunita all through elementary school—calling the Sen family sinister, or sinful, or senseless, or some other silly adjective. Usually Sunita took it good-naturedly, but this time she didn't smile. John's

105

teasing had sometimes bordered on the edge of being mean, which made him a prime suspect in her hunt for the voice that had whispered behind her and Ilana that day.

"We're not asking for anything from you, John," she answered coolly. John looked surprised and a bit hurt.

The bell rang, and Mr. Riley began writing on the board. Sunita was becoming more and more thankful for teachers. If only school were continuous classes and lectures. Then she wouldn't have to deal with her classmates.

"What's with Sunni?" she overhead John whisper to Jeannie.

"Not too sunny anymore, is she?" Jeannie whispered back.

The week before Halloween went from bad to worse. Sunita, who used to bounce out of bed in the morning anticipating another day of school, began to dread it more each day. A cool, haughty Sunita seemed to switch on as soon as she got on the school bus and wouldn't switch off until she got home at the end of the day. She felt more and more distant from the people she'd grown up with, and she knew most of them were noticing it.

Except Michael. He probably wouldn't notice if she stopped going to school altogether. He was deep into his own world of tennis, tennis, and more tennis. He had even started practicing serves during lunch. Which of course meant that LeAnn led her crowd of followers out to the bleachers to watch him.

And Liz was no longer the same old comfortable Liz. She'd become part of Liz 'n' Bill. He and Liz spent each lunch hour analyzing their last track meet. Instead of sitting in the cafeteria with them, Sunita began slipping into the school library to forget herself in a book. But she always made sure she stayed far away from the group huddled in front of the *Star Trek* videos.

When the weekend finally came, Sunita felt as if she was on temporary parole. No school for three whole days. Dad had booked rooms at the Ahwahnee Hotel for two nights and had informed Sunita she could miss school on Monday just this once.

Early Saturday morning, before the sun had risen over the hills, the Sens packed the car and drove off. Even Geetie put away her books, picket signs, and petitions to come along, squashed in the back seat with Sunita, her mom, and her grandmother. As the oldest member of the family, Dadu rode in the front passenger seat and was given the responsibility of holding Dad's collection of maps.

Sunita felt strangely peaceful as the car pulled away from their neighborhood and headed toward the mountains. She joined in the Bengali song that Dadu had started, loudly singing the phrase or two she knew and humming the rest.

Chapter 14

Yosemite National Park was everything Dad had hoped it would be. Autumn colors filled the valley, and the Sens took long, quiet walks by themselves on the usually overcrowded trails. All around them were "signs of God's majesty," as Dadu put it—towering redwoods, waterfalls, the high, rocky Sierras, and meadows full of wildflowers.

"You have two marvelous institutions in America that you must never take for granted," he told his granddaughters. "One is the public library system. And the other is your national parks and forests."

Sunita felt rejuvenated and hopeful when they headed back to town late Monday night. This week had to be better than last week, she thought. Anything would be an improvement.

When the car turned onto their street, Dad groaned. Their entire house was decked with yards and yards of toilet paper. The culprits had even hopped the fence and plastered the back of the house with it. Their tennis shoes had trampled all over the tiny plants that were springing up. Dadu's face was grim as he surveyed the damage.

Suddenly, Sunita remembered John Rostowski's promise of a Halloween trick. She wondered which of LeAnn's groupies had joined him. John couldn't have done all of it alone. Had Michael been one of the kids that had leapt the fence and destroyed Dadu's garden?

When Sunita walked into social studies class on Tuesday morning, she glared at each of her classmates in turn. Which of them had been there? Which of them were responsible for her grandfather's sorrow? And she was still on the hunt for the whisperer. By second period, all of them were keeping their distance from Sunita—except Liz, who stuck to her side like a loyal leech. And Bill McTaggart, of course, who had forgotten that he could exist apart from Liz.

At lunch, Liz managed to peel away from him and join Sunita in the library.

"I've got the scoop," she said. "It was Rostowski all right. He and LeAnn and Jeannie and a bunch of others did the front yard, just as a joke. But I guess a gang of high school guys joined them and sort of commandeered the whole thing. Michael had nothing to do with it."

"I'll bet," said Sunita sarcastically. "He'd do anything LeAnn Schaeffer told him to do. I have a feeling she's behind the whole thing."

Liz stood up, slowly. "It's not like you to be so small, Sunita Sen," she said. Her green eyes were full of reproach. "You know, Michael might not be spending quite as much time with LeAnn if you hadn't been so cold to him. Quit feeling so sorry for yourself."

So for the rest of the day, even Liz deserted her. Sunita held on to her anger, kept her head high, and held back the tears until school was over. She hurried into Geetie's room as soon as she got home.

Mom tapped softly on the door. "Bontu? Can I come in?"

Didn't she have any privacy? Was there nowhere to escape?

"I'm trying to be alone," she said.

"I'll leave you alone," answered Mom. "I promise. I need to get a sweater for Didu out of Geetie's closet."

Sunita grabbed her notebook, stormed past her mother, and headed out to the back yard. At the far end of the yard, her grandfather turned and lifted his hand in greeting. The air was chilly, and Sunita dragged an old lawn chair out from the shade of the plum trees into the sunshine.

She watched her grandfather painstakingly cleaning the yard and propping up the crocuses and felt mad at her classmates all over again. All day, underneath her anger, she had secretly enjoyed shattering her bland image. An angry Sunita was an enigma to them. "Cheerful." "Always Happy." "Bouncy and Sweet." That's how they'd described her in last year's yearbook. But not this year. She had finally become a woman of mystery.

Her family was just as baffled by her behavior at home. The very sight of her mother made Sunita grumpy. Somehow, she couldn't stop feeling that this entire mess was Mom's fault. If Mom would go back to being herself, maybe Sunita's life would straighten out somehow.

Sunita suddenly realized that her grandfather was leaning on his spade and watching her. She leaned over her notebook so that he couldn't see her face.

"Why so downcast, my granddaughter?" he asked. His voice was tender, and he bent over so that he could see her eyes.

Sunita wondered why it was his kindness that brought the tears. Her grandfather wiped the soil from his fingers on his dhoti and handed her a clean, white handkerchief. He stood beside Sunita, letting her cry without saying a word. Somehow, his quiet presence was comforting, and she stopped after a while.

"May I recite a poem for you?" he asked then.

"I guess so," answered Sunita, blowing her nose on his handkerchief.

"This is written by Rabindranath Tagore, the famous Bengali poet who won the Nobel Prize for literature."

"I didn't know a Bengali Indian had ever won the Nobel Prize," said Sunita. She had always thought she'd be the first one. When she couldn't fall asleep at night, she'd lie awake composing the speech she'd make when she won the Pulitzer or Nobel Prize. *She is wearing a glittery, low-cut evening gown. A tuxedoed, slightly graying at the temples Michael look-alike is clapping vigorously in the audience . . .*

With a jolt, she realized that she still had Michael playing a lead role in the life of Sunita Sen. Even though he'd permanently resigned. Dadu cleared his throat to get her attention. "Ready?" he asked.

"Ready," she answered.

On many an idle day have I grieved over lost time.
But it is never lost, my Lord. Thou hast taken every
moment of my life in thine own hands.
Hidden in the heart of things thou art nourishing
seeds into sprouts, buds into blossoms, and ripening
flowers into fruitfulness.
I was tired and sleeping on my bed and imagined all
work had ceased. In the morning I woke and found
my garden full with wonders of flowers.

When Dadu's singsong voice stopped, he dropped a kiss on the top of her head and went inside.

Sunita sat quietly for a long time, thinking. Then she got up and marched over to the rocky soil.

It wasn't fair. All the seeds deserved just as much of a chance at becoming full-fledged flowers as the ones in the good soil. Sunita's observation experiment was about to take a new, unscientific turn. *"Hidden in the heart of things . . . ,"* she repeated to herself as she ruthlessly began clearing away pebbles.

Chapter 15

"I am so excited that Ajit can come home for the Bengali celebration this year," Mom said one Saturday over lunch. "He'll spend the whole weekend with us. It's the weekend of the Berkeley-Stanford Big Game. I thought you girls could go to the game by train, and then all three of you can come home together in his car. Then on Sunday, we'll take two cars to the celebration."

Both Sunita and Geetie looked up. Their eyes met across the table. You first, Sunita signaled silently.

"Are you becoming senile, Mother?" Geetie asked.

Sunita winced at her sister's opening statement. Geetie was forgetting all the basics about diplomacy.

Her sister continued. "You perpetually forget that I am a vegetarian. Now you don't seem to care at all that I am a pacifist. Football is a barbaric game, and there is no way I am going to the Big Game this year."

Mom looked troubled.

"I thought that since Maria was a cheerleader this year, you'd want to go to at least one game," she said.

"That's exactly why I do not want to go. I will not watch my best friend become an object for the pleasure of men."

"Okay, Sangita," Dad said. "We know all about your high moral principles. You don't have to go. Bontu can take Liz, and they can meet Ajit there."

Dad's assumption that she would go without Geetie irritated Sunita. Didn't she have any control over her own life? Was everything to be decided by them? Sunita decided that she too was through with diplomacy.

"I, for one, am not going to that Indian thing this year," she announced.

Everybody stared at her. Sunita had even surprised herself. She hadn't planned on not attending the festival. It was a big annual family event. All the Bay Area Bengali families would meet in some musty community center, festoon it with Indian decorations, and fill it with savory smells rising from huge pots of curry.

"You've always enjoyed the festival, Bontu," said Mom. "And your grandparents are here this year. Why don't you want to go?"

"I brought you a beautiful new saree from India to wear, Bontu," added Didu. "And gorgeous jewels and gold bangles. Everybody will admire you."

"You can't bribe me to go," said Sunita scornfully. "I'm not going. And that's final."

Even Geetie raised her eyebrows at Sunita's tone of voice.

Their grandmother gasped. "Such rudeness!" she said, shaking her head woefully. "You should have listened to me, Arun. I warned you and Ranee that America would ruin the children."

Dad turned to Sunita.

"You'll do as we tell you, daughter," he said in Bengali. Sunita knew he was upset when he spoke to her in Bengali. "You will go with us to the festival. Now go to your room."

Sunita fled. About twenty minutes later, she heard Mom's gentle knock. Sunita grabbed a book so that Mom would think she'd been reading.

"Come in," she said.

Mom was carrying a gleaming pile of purple silk in one hand and a pair of golden sandals in the other. "Won't you at least try on the saree Didu bought for you, Bontu? It would make her so happy if you did."

Suddenly, her mother's gentle voice with its lilting Indian accent seemed to grate on Sunita's ears. And how she despised that infernal dot on her mother's forehead.

"My name is not BONTU!" she shouted. "It is SUNITA. I will never wear one of those long sheets in public. If YOU want to be elected Indian woman of the year or something, just go right ahead, but LEAVE ME OUT OF IT!"

Mom stood in the doorway for a while without saying anything, staring at her daughter.

When she finally spoke, her voice sounded sad and her words surprised Sunita. "I forget that you're not a little girl anymore," she said. "Someday you may wish you had made different choices. But I suppose, in a way, you're right. You need to find your own balance, and I need to find mine."

Dad's knock came a few minutes later, and it sounded more like pounding than knocking. Sunita opened the door reluctantly.

He was upset, all right. "Your behavior today has been atrocious, young lady. Don't ever let me hear you shouting at your mother like that again. And let me tell you once again, in case you didn't hear me earlier—you are joining the rest of the family at that festival."

Sunita was her father's daughter. "You'll have to carry me there," she said, folding her arms across her chest. They glared at each other.

Suddenly, a shriek came from outside. It was Didu. Sunita followed Dad as he raced downstairs. Mom and Geetie were close behind him. They were all thinking the same thing—Dadu had been working hard, long hours restoring the garden. Had something happened to him?

But the shriek hadn't come from the garden. Didu, her arms wrapped around Dadu, was jumping up and down beside the mailbox. Bills and letters were strewn all over the driveway.

"What happened? Who should I call? Fire? Ambulance? Police?" Dad gasped, out of breath.

"No, no, Arun, relax," said Dadu, disentangling himself from his wife's enthusiastic embrace. "It seems that my Ria has just received a letter informing her that she has won first prize in the *Endless Hope* contest."

Didu waved the letter. She was speechless with delight.

"Oh, my" was all Dad could say. He planted himself on the curb. One by one, Sunita, Mom, and Geetie joined him. Of all the reasons for Didu's unearthly shriek, this was something that hadn't occurred to any of them.

Dadu's eyes twinkled as he surveyed the blank faces of the four Sens. "Your grandmother used to win essay competitions all the time in school," he told them.

"Are they really sending you to New York for a weekend?" Geetie asked.

"I don't know," Didu answered. "I was too excited to read past 'Congratulations. You have won our first-ever *Endless Hope* plot solution contest.' Here, Arun. You find out the details."

Dad scanned the letter. "Yes. If you want, you can actually arrive on the Friday when they begin taping the shows with your suggestions. If not, you can go any weekend of your choice. Let's see—your first show will be taped in two weeks."

"Oh, we have to go then," Didu said. "We are free, aren't we, Ranee darling?"

"Of course you are, Ma. That's the weekend of the Bengali festival, but this is far more important."

Sunita gave Dad a triumphant look. If they didn't have to go, she certainly shouldn't have to go. As they headed back into the house to celebrate over tea, Dad swatted Sunita on the head with the bills.

"I suppose we'll all skip the festival this year and enjoy a quiet weekend at home," he said. "But be careful, daughter of mine. I'll be keeping a close eye on you."

Chapter 16

Dad gave his daughter warning looks every now and then, but from that day on, Mom honored a hands-off policy. She always called her Sunita and never Bontu. She stopped reminding her to kiss her grandparents every night, go over her homework with Dadu, help him in the garden, or make conversation at dinner. She even stopped inviting Sunita to accompany them on outings.

Sunita tried to tell herself that she finally felt free. But all she could feel was . . . off balance. She'd been doing great in school ever since Dadu had been reviewing her work with her. He even made math interesting. Rubbing the back of his head ruefully, he'd described how his brother used to keep him awake to study math: "He tied one end of a string around a lock of my hair and the other end to the chair. When my head dropped forward, the string pulled me awake with a mighty tug."

If Dadu wondered why Sunita didn't kiss him good night anymore or bring her homework to him each night, he didn't say anything. But his welcome in the garden was just as hearty and their conversations just as interesting. Sunita was grateful that her experiment lasted all semester. Making sure Mom would see the notebook in her hands, she was still able to spend time in the back yard after school.

In fact, with all the effort it took to be cold and reserved at school and cold and grumpy at home, the garden was the only place Sunita felt like herself now. It was a safe place, a place to write, a place to be quiet if she wanted, a place to daydream, and a place to feel the encircling love of her grandfather.

She knew that when Dadu came to join her for a rest, he would sense that she didn't want to talk about herself. He wouldn't ask any silly probing questions. He might stay quiet as they watched twilight settle on the garden. Or he might tell her stories—funny stories from his childhood, exciting stories from his college days, and glorious old fables about the kings and empires of ancient India. She'd like to give Dadu a story about himself as a present, she thought.

When he talked about his childhood, she could almost feel the heat of the noonday sun pouring onto the jute fields in the Indian countryside, smell the ripe mangoes strewn on either side of the path to school, and hear the lazy sounds of the crows in the afternoon. She moved her chair back into the sunshine, out of the reach of the lengthening shadows, shut her eyes, and tried to picture him as a boy growing up in the Indian countryside.

The winding dirt path leads through the mango trees. Soft shafts of sunlight filtering through the trees have dried some of the flatter parts of the ground. The boy's cycle speeds easily over the path, avoiding holes and muddy puddles as though it doesn't need his help. It stops obediently when he spots a ripe orange mango lying on the side of the path. He peels its thin skin off with his teeth and lets the sweet juice fill his mouth.

He cycles through the mango grove to the river. The current is fast and a bit wild after the rains. A small rope bridge made of jute hangs across the surface of the water, and the boy balances his cycle on his shoulder as he crosses it. He is thin, but his arms and legs are wiry. His father grows the jute plants on their land, and the boy feels pride in the strength of the tightly woven rope made from its fibers.

On the other side of the river, he leans the cycle against the bank and runs back to the middle of the rope, enjoying the feel of the cool water pouring over his bare feet. He squints into the sunshine and watches the silver river curve through the green rice paddies.

The house is only a short distance from the river.

He lets his cycle fall in the soft dirt near the flower garden and runs to the water pump. There is a full bucket of cool bath water waiting for him.

After bathing, he refills the bucket with several smooth swings of the pump handle. He dresses in clean clothes that have dried on the line in the sunshine, combs his hair, and runs into the kitchen to see his mother and sisters.

His father and elder brother come in from their work, freshly bathed and hungry. After eating the midday meal, the family rests together on jute mats. Outside, the land is still and bright and hot. But inside the clay house, the floor is cool, and a soft light comes through the faded cotton cloths that hang across the open windows. The familiar sounds of men praying and chanting in the mosque are faint and far away.

The boy wakes to the clatter of the tea kettle. He grabs his cricket bat and ball and runs out to play cricket with the boys who till and harvest his father's jute. They shout and play together until they can no longer see the ball in the twilight.

He walks home alone through the tall grasses and wildflowers. To the west, the leaves of the palm trees are black against the soft gold of the sky. The boy can hear his mother singing as she combs out his grandmother's long gray hair on the balcony of the house. Every evening, he stops to listen to her sing as the last light fades.

123

"Come in and start studying right now!" his brother calls into the darkness. "Your examinations are next month." The boy slowly turns his face away from the western sky and runs toward the love he hears in his brother's voice.

After scribbling the beginnings of Dadu's story in her journal, Sunita remembered that she hadn't taken observation notes on her experiment. With a sigh, she started her daily round of the four types of soil.

Her grandfather stood beside her as she scowled over the thriving flowers in the good soil. The special care she had lavished on the seeds in the three other types of soil had been wasted. Only a few flowers had survived in each.

"You must understand the point of the parable, Bontu," Dadu said suddenly. "Remember that soil has no control over the seeds that are sown in it. How would you describe the soil's job?"

"I don't think soil has much of a job," Sunita answered. "It's just a bunch of dirt."

"That is where you are wrong, Bontu. The soil's job is to receive and nurture whatever seeds are sown. Only then come the fruits and flowers. What do you think the different types of soils are meant to represent?" he asked.

This time, she thought for a minute before answering. "I suppose different types of people, or hearts, or something like that."

He smiled, delighted by her answer. "Exactly! We are the soil, Bontu, you and I. We have no control over which seeds are sown in our lives. But we can become good soil, receive gratefully the seeds given, and nurture them until we see fruit."

That was all he said, but Sunita wrote the gist of it in her journal later. She might need to explain it to her grandchildren some day.

Chapter 17

" I have a favor to ask, Geetie," Sunita said. The sisters had fallen into the habit of talking for a while after they turned the lights off in their room.

"What is it?"

Sunita hesitated and took a deep breath. "Won't you go with me to the Big Game this weekend?" she asked.

Last year, she had visited A.J., worn red, and rooted for Stanford. This year, the game was at Berkeley, and she wanted to sit on the Berkeley side to watch Maria leading cheers.

Maria had phoned Sunita that afternoon before Geetie got home.

"You've got to talk her into coming to the game, Sunni," Maria had pleaded. "You're my only hope. She hates to say no to you."

"She does?" asked Sunita. "I didn't think anybody could sway Geetie once she's made up her mind. Well, I'll give it a try."

She'd put it off until now. There was something intimate about the darkness that made it easier to ask.

"You know how I feel, Bontu," Geetie answered. "You heard what I told Mom the other day."

"You can't let your convictions ruin your friendship with Maria. I think Maria's hurt that you don't want to watch her lead cheers."

"She hasn't even noticed that I haven't come to the games, I bet. She's too busy with silly sorority parties and empty-headed fraternity boys. Plus being a sex object on campus."

"She probably thinks you're too involved in your protests and boycotts to care about her. Besides, Liz can't go with me. Mom and Dad won't let me go alone, and I really want to to. Please, Geetie."

Geetie was silent for a while. Then she sighed—an exasperated, resigned sigh. "Are you really going to make me watch a bunch of dumb guys knock each other out, and a bunch of girls in tight sweaters jumping up and down?"

Sunita nodded vigorously, even though her sister couldn't see her. "Yup. And we'll get to see A.J. at the game," she reminded Geetie.

"That's true. Old happy-go-lucky always cheers

me up. Okay, Bontu," said Geetie. "Now go to sleep before you ask me to compromise any more of my principles."

"Okay, Geetie," said Sunita meekly. "Thanks a lot."

She smiled to herself in the darkness. Maria would be delighted, and Sunita finally had a good excuse to skip the all-county juniors tennis tournament scheduled for the coming weekend. Michael was ranked third, which was surprising for the youngest player in the whole tournament. Half the school was turning out to cheer him on, and Liz had been dropping hints all week to Sunita about it. But there was no way Sunita was going to endure watching LeAnn sit cozily next to "Kate," squealing each time Michael hit the ball.

The weekend of the Big Game and the Big Adventure to New York came quickly, with all the excitement of getting Didu and Dadu ready for their Thursday evening departure. When Dad and Mom got back from the airport, they looked exhausted.

Sunita noticed that both of her parents slept in on Friday morning. Dad must have been extremely late to work, because he hadn't emerged by the time Sunita left for school. On Friday afternoon, Mom went to aerobics for the first time in months. The Sens had a pizza and sushi meal that night, served on paper plates. And Dad brought home theater tickets for two to a Saturday matinee in San Francisco.

Early Saturday afternoon, Sunita sat on the steps of Sproul Hall on the Berkeley campus, watching students dressed in blue and gold walk toward the football stadium. A cold wind was sweeping across the bay, and she pulled her Berkeley sweatshirt tightly around her. Geetie had run into the library for "twenty minutes." She'd already been gone for over an hour.

A group of African students dressed in brightly colored shirts came out of Sproul Hall, intently discussing some issue in another language. One of them almost tripped over Sunita.

"So sorry, mademoiselle," he said.

Sunita watched them disappear into the crowd of people milling around the plaza. She felt a pang of envy. African on the outside and African on the inside. Nice and simple. Like Liz and Michael. And LeAnn. White—oops, she meant Euro-American—on the outside, and Euro-American on the inside.

Geetie had lectured the whole family one day, reminding them that *American* and *white* were not the same thing. "The correct term," she'd announced, "is Euro-American."

Was there a correct term for someone like Sunita Sen? On the outside, an Indian body dressed in American clothes. On the inside, total confusion.

She stood up and spotted Geetie talking to a guy strumming a guitar. The guy shook his head, and his matted locks of hair swung back and forth. Geetie shrugged and lifted her hands helplessly.

Sunita walked over to them, worried that Geetie was going to back out at the last minute. "I hope you're proud of yourself" was Geetie's greeting. "Tom couldn't believe that you talked a total pacifist into going to a football game. But even he says I should go once—just for the experience."

Sunita smiled gratefully at Tom, who twanged a mournful-sounding chord on his guitar in reply. Linking her arm through her sister's, Sunita drew them into the crowd of students heading toward the football stadium.

"Where did Maria say to sit?" she asked her sister.

"I guess some of her friends are saving us seats in the front of the student section," answered Geetie, putting on a pair of dark sunglasses. "But let's just sit up in the back."

"No way," answered Sunita. "When A.J. comes over from the Stanford side, he'll never see us way up there. And what do you need those dark glasses for? It's totally cloudy today."

Firmly, she headed toward the front. When they got there, Sunita scanned the field for the group of cheerleaders.

"Maria!" she yelled, and waved furiously. Geetie

pulled the hood of her sweatshirt over her head and shrank down into it.

One of the figures in a pleated gold and blue skirt and a clingy sweater broke away from the group and ran toward them, waving a pom-pom.

"Hi, Geetie! Hi, Sunita!" From the relieved smile on Maria's face, Sunita could tell she wasn't the only one who'd worried about Geetie backing out at the last minute.

"Where do we sit?" asked Sunita.

"Some of my sorority sisters are saving seats for you right up there." Maria pointed with her pom-pom, and a couple of girls waved back. "They're sitting with a few fraternity brothers. There's one I really want you to meet, Geetie. His name's Mark Takahashi. Try to be civil to him. For my sake, okay?"

Geetie groaned, and Maria winked at Sunita.

"See you after the game," she said, running back to the cheerleaders' circle of blue and gold.

The sisters pushed their way past knees and elbows to their seats. When they sat down, Sunita noticed that her sister was sitting beside a guy wearing a fraternity sweatshirt.

He leaned over to introduce himself. "I'm Mark."

Geetie nodded. Sunita gave her sister a sharp elbow. "Take off your hood," she hissed. "And those silly glasses."

For the whole first half of the game, Geetie sat stiffly away from the guy beside her, who made one or two friendly comments.

Once or twice, Sunita's mind drifted away from the game, and she caught herself wondering whether Michael was winning the tournament. But at halftime, Sunita kept a close eye on the cheerleaders during their routines. Maria was the smallest girl, so she was flipped and tossed around the most. Students threw confetti all over the stands.

"That's the first thing I'm going to change," Sunita heard the guy sitting beside her sister mutter. "What a waste!"

"What's a waste?" she asked, leaning over Geetie.

"I've just started a position as campus recycling coordinator," he answered. "All this confetti's got to go."

Geetie pulled off her glasses and turned to face him.

"So you're the guy who's taking Mitchell's place. It didn't take us too long to get rid of him. I have a ton of questions for you."

Stanford beat Berkeley at the last minute, 28–21. A.J. had joined his sisters on the Berkeley side for the last quarter. He'd carefully removed all the red and white he'd been wearing so that nobody on the Berkeley side would know he was a Stanford fan. But he couldn't restrain himself after the last touchdown and almost got thrown over the railing when he stood up to cheer wildly.

Everyone who attended the game would remember it as one of the most exciting Big Games in history. Especially Geetie and Mark, who spent the entire second half of the game debating the pros and cons of three different recycling programs.

"Who won?" asked Mark, looking up at the scoreboard as A.J. shielded himself behind Sunita. Berkeley fans were throwing empty popcorn containers, crumpled programs, and other people's shoes at him as they exited the stadium.

"Is it over?" asked Geetie, staring around her as though she'd forgotten they were in the stadium.

When Maria came up to join them, Geetie was absorbed in a detailed account of an expedition Mark had taken to the Brazilian rain forests. Sunita watched the smile of pleasure spread across Maria's face.

"Why don't you stay for the party, Geetie?" asked Maria. "Mark's frat is hosting it."

"I'm driving Bontu home, Geetie, so you don't have to worry about her," A.J. added, putting his arm around Sunita. "I'll even pick you up at the train station tonight. Last train leaves at midnight, I think."

Geetie looked over at Mark, who was collecting piles of trash with a concerned look on his face.

"Okay," she said, bending down to start helping him.

"Do you have a car here, Mark?" asked Maria. "It looks like it might rain, and we need a ride over to the sorority house."

"Sorry, Maria," he answered. "You know I don't own a car. Never have and never will. I bike everywhere I go."

Sunita couldn't help grinning at her sister, who made sure Mark wasn't looking and grinned back.

Chapter 18

Michael won the tournament. The local paper's sports section had a big photo spread on his five-set victory match. As soon as A.J. left on Sunday, Sunita grabbed the paper and closeted herself in the den. Geetie was still fast asleep in their room, snoring blissfully.

The article made it seem as if Michael Morrison was the town's best hope to make it on the international map. There was even an interview with his parents. Every photo of Michael made Sunita's heart jump.

She'd been trying to forget how much the sight of him still hurt. They hadn't talked in weeks. And she had missed the best tennis that he'd ever played—better than either of them had anticipated in the summer.

Suddenly, she realized that it had been a long

time since she'd played tennis herself. When the girls' season came around in the spring, she didn't want to lose out on the number one slot. It was a beautiful, sunny day. She grabbed her racket and a bucket of balls and headed over to the park. She could at least hit against the backboard for a while if she couldn't find a partner.

At the park, only one court was being used—by the county tournament champ himself, Michael Morrison, in person, without any of his entourage around to cheer him on. He was rallying with Kevin Chang.

Kevin was the most unfailingly cheerful person Sunita knew. Her coldness to one and all over the past few weeks at school hadn't dimmed Kevin's enthusiastic greeting every time he saw her.

"Hellooooo, Sunitita Chiquitita!" he yodeled now, before she could slip past them. "My lady in shining armor. You're here just in the nick of time. Could you step in for me for just a bit? I have to go check that my kid brother is still alive somewhere around here."

Sunita looked across the court at Michael, who was studying his racket strings intently. Kevin tossed her the balls he was holding.

"I'll be right back, I promise," he said. There was nothing else to do. She picked up the balls and unzipped her racket cover.

What she liked best about playing tennis with

Michael was that he never took it easy on her. What he liked best about playing with her was that she was consistent. She could hit shot after shot to his backhand, placing the ball to the left of him every time. They slipped into their old rallying routine without a word—forehand crosscourts, followed by backhand crosscourts, approach shots, lobs, and so on.

After a while, Sunita began wondering whether Kevin would ever come back. And whether she wanted him to. It was so nice to be playing tennis with Michael again.

Suddenly, there was Kevin, clutching a screaming toddler version of himself.

"The little guy skinned his knee," Kevin told Michael and Sunita. "I've got to go patch him up. Sorry, Morrison. See you guys tomorrow."

After Kevin left, Michael walked over to the bench and sat down. Sunita joined him.

"Do you want to keep hitting?" he asked. "Don't feel like you have to."

"No, it's okay. This is great practice for me."

"I haven't seen you on the courts in a while," he said. She noticed that his voice was guarded, and that he didn't look at her face.

"I've been busy."

"So I've noticed."

They were quiet for a while. The sunshine made it seem like summer, but every now and then a chilly wind shook down some leaves onto the courts. Sunita pulled on her sweatshirt.

"Congratulations on the tournament," she said.

"Thanks," he answered.

She didn't know what to say next. The park had never seemed so empty and quiet.

"Michael—" she started.

"Sunni—" he said at the same time.

They smiled.

"You first," she said.

"It feels like summer today, doesn't it?" he asked.

"That's exactly what I was going to say!" she said, amazed.

"It makes me thirsty for lemonade," he said.

She smiled, remembering the lemonade they used to make in the kitchen. They'd argue over how much sugar to add and taste it so often that there was hardly enough left for two glasses when they were done.

Suddenly, she remembered that Didu and Dadu were in New York. Maybe Mom's rule about boys didn't apply this weekend. Taking a deep breath, she decided to risk it.

"Maybe we can make some at our place," she said.

He looked surprised. "I don't want to bother your family, especially with your grandparents here and all. They're probably resting or something."

"They're gone. My grandmother won some soap

opera contest, and they flew her and my grand-father to New York City for the weekend."

"Really?" he asked. "It wasn't that *Endless Hope* contest, was it?"

"It was! How in the world did you hear about it?"

He grinned. "My grandmother never misses a show. She'll want to meet your grandmother for sure."

Sunita decided it was time to change the subject. "Tell me about the tournament, Michael. I want to hear every detail."

When they got to the Sens' house, he was in the middle of describing the intense quarterfinal match. Sunita hoped he didn't notice how surprised her parents looked when they saw him. Thankfully, Mom was wearing sweats, and there was no sign of the dot on her forehead. The house looked clut-tered as usual, though, with the Sunday paper strewn all over the living room and Dad lounging on the sofa.

"Good afternoon, Mr. and Mrs. Sen," Michael said. He was always impeccably courteous to grown-ups.

"We were just reading about your tremendous victory, Michael. Congratulations!" said Sunita's dad.

"Thanks, sir," Michael answered. "I know Sunita will do just as well in the junior girls' tournament this spring."

"If you keep her practicing, she might have a shot at it," Mom said, smiling.

Sunita felt a surge of irritation. How hypocritical, she thought. First Mom warns Sunita not to taint the family reputation by bringing a member of the opposite sex to the house. Then she practically begs Michael to spend time with her unpopular daughter.

"Let's go, Michael," Sunita said, giving her mother a disgusted look. They headed to the kitchen to make some lemonade.

Mom's voice followed them down the hall. "What did I say, Arun? What could I possibly have said?" Embarrassed, Sunita shut the kitchen door behind them.

Michael spent the whole afternoon at the Sens'. They played Ping-Pong for a while, and she taught Michael how to play Carom. Then she took him outside to show off Dadu's garden. As he admired the order and beauty that Dadu had created, Sunita realized how silly she'd been to suspect him of the damage done on Halloween.

They sat on the lawn furniture, side by side. This time their silence was a comfortable one. Something about the peace of the garden gave Sunita courage.

"Michael, I need to tell you something," she said suddenly.

He turned to face her. "What is it, Sunni?"

"I know I've been acting crazy."

"Yes," he said. "You certainly have been."

140

"Do you remember when you wanted to come over at the end of last summer and I sort of—avoided the subject?"

"That day in the park? I sure do."

She took a deep breath and started talking fast. "My grandparents had just arrived from India, and my mom was freaking out trying to be all Indian for them or something, and she asked me not to invite boys over, and I thought you'd think that was dumb so—"

She stopped. He was quiet. "So you avoided me and didn't tell me the truth," he said finally, finishing the sentence for her. "That stinks, Sunni. What kind of a jerk do you think I am?"

"Don't be mad, Michael. I don't think you're a jerk at all. I thought you'd think *I* was a jerk because my family's so strange."

He shook his head. "Wait. Wait. Let me get this straight. For all these weeks, you've been acting strange because you thought I would think your family's strange." He groaned. "Why are women so complicated?"

She giggled. It felt so good to tell him the truth. "I'm sorry, Michael. Liz was right. I should have told you the truth from the start."

She considered asking him about LeAnn, and then decided not to. He was perfectly free to spend time with LeAnn Schaeffer if he wanted to. Sunita Sen was not about to expose any signs of jealousy.

141

"So when can I start coming over?" he asked. "The sooner your grandparents observe my angelic behavior the better. It won't take them long to see that you need my good influence."

"I'll have to wait and see what Mom says." She still couldn't picture Michael actually meeting her grandparents.

Michael got up to leave. "I'm glad I came over," he said. "Your mom needs a reminder of my spotless character. She's sure to change her mind."

Michael looked smugly over at Sunita when her mom invited him to join them for dinner. "No thanks, Mrs. Sen," he said. "We're having dinner guests. But I'll definitely take a rain check."

Sunita walked him out to the porch, wondering if LeAnn was becoming a regular Sunday night guest at the Morrisons'.

"I'm sure glad Kevin Chang has a little brother," he said. "See you tomorrow, Sunni."

She wandered back into the house, humming the theme song from *Casablanca*.

Chapter 19

"**Y**ou *what*?!" Liz leaned over her desk, clutching her chest.

"Shhh. Keep it down, Liz. I told him the truth," Sunita whispered back. The two girls had come in early to the social studies classroom so they could talk. Mr. Riley was in front, scribbling on the board.

"I'm so proud of you, Sunni," Liz said. "I knew you'd come through eventually. So when can he go over and meet your grandparents? It'll be love at first sight on both sides, just you wait and see."

"Mom's rule still stands, you know."

"Why don't you ask her? I'll bet she changes her mind."

"Well . . . I think I'll wait."

Sunita didn't want to admit how uncomfortable

she still felt about Michael meeting Didu and Dadu. Not even to Liz.

The bell rang, and the other students drifted in. Michael came in, with LeAnn right behind him. He stopped by Sunita's desk.

"That was the best lemonade I've tasted all year, Sunni," he said.

Sunita felt better. The way to a man's heart is through his stomach, Didu had told her once. LeAnn Schaeffer might be gorgeous, but Sunita Sen made a great glass of lemonade.

In fact, it was the best she had felt in a long time. Telling Michael the truth had been such a relief. She felt as if a weight had been lifted off her shoulders. She actually laughed at one of John Rostowski's dumb jokes.

She was even looking forward to going home. Mom had been normal all weekend long—no sarees, no dot, no cooking for hours on end. But when Sunita got home, she realized Mom's relapse into her old, relaxed self had been temporary. Didu and Dadu were coming back that night, and Mom cooked curry, lit an incense stick, and put on her full garb before leaving for the airport.

Sunita's grandparents burst into the house, wearing matching extra-large promotional T-shirts that said "Endlessly Hoping in New York." Didu wore hers over a saree. She was bubbling with excitement. The *Endless Hope* writers had been working like mad on her plot solution, and the first show was to be aired the following week. They were even including her name in the credits—Ria Majumdar, Idea Editor.

In four days, Sunita's grandparents had visited every tourist spot in the city, from the World Trade Center to Central Park to Fifth Avenue.

Dadu had been most impressed by the Statue of Liberty. "What a lady," he told Sunita. "There she stands, regally, welcoming one and all. This nation of immigrants has no grander symbol."

Sunita was surprised at how glad she was to see them. But her irritation with Mom mounted. Even Didu was becoming more Americanized, for heaven's sake. Why couldn't Mom lighten up a bit?

There was still no way that she was going to be seen with a saree-clad mom in public. And that meant the end of a special Thanksgiving weekend tradition that they shared with Liz and Mrs. Grayson. Each year, the girls were allowed to spend money on one out-of-the-ordinary item at the mall. Their mothers met them afterward, and the four of them headed off for high tea at the fanciest hotel in town. Mr. Grayson had dubbed it "Tea for Four" and grumbled every year that it would send him to the poorhouse.

This year, Sunita told Mrs. Grayson that her mom was too busy with Didu and Dadu to come. "We'll have to call it off," she said.

"Are you sure?" Mrs. Grayson asked. "It seems a shame to stop our lovely tradition."

She looked so sad that Sunita repented a bit. "We don't need to stop it totally, Mrs. Grayson. Maybe you, Liz, and I can still go to the mall that day. We'll just skip the tea part."

Sunita didn't say anything to Mom about canceling Tea for Four. She decided she would let Mom bring it up, and then tell her the truth—that she was embarrassed to be seen in the mall with a mother dressed like an alien. Maybe then Mom would wear one of her cute outfits, and the four of them could go out as they used to.

But as the days went by, Mom didn't bring it up. By Thanksgiving weekend, Sunita was crushed. Wouldn't Mrs. Grayson have mentioned it to Mom? The two of them talked on the phone at least once a week. Maybe Mom really was too distracted this year to remember. Or care.

Mom didn't even say anything when the Graysons' car honked for Sunita on Saturday.

"I have to run some errands, girls," said Mrs. Grayson, dropping them off at the mall. "Meet me by Macy's at three, okay? And don't forget about the time in a bookstore somewhere, Elizabeth."

Sunita smiled to herself as she climbed out of the car. Liz's mother knew her daughter so well. The way Mom used to know me, she thought with a pang.

Inside, Sunita pushed a reluctant Liz toward the jewelry store.

"You won't regret this, Liz. I promise," she urged, wondering if she could really convince her friend to go through with it.

Looking terrified, Liz clutched her earlobes as they entered the store. Suddenly, Sunita stopped, forgetting her mission for a moment. Ilana Taylor was inside, trying on bracelets. She nodded coolly as Liz and Sunita walked in.

Unknowingly, Liz broke the ice. "Hi, Ilana. Don't be surprised if you hear bloodcurdling shrieks echoing through the mall. Sunni's forcing me to get my ears pierced."

"Really? I'm thinking about getting another hole in each ear," Ilana told her. "But I have to convince my parents first."

"You mean to say that you've endured this barbaric torture twice and you'd go through it again?" Liz asked, looking incredulously at the two golden hoops dangling from each of Ilana's ears.

Sunita decided it was a teachable moment.

"Take a look in the mirror over there, Liz," she said, spinning her friend around and giving Ilana a significant look. "Your ears look naked next to Ilana's. Stark naked. Don't they, Ilana?"

Ilana seemed surprised for a moment, but then she caught on. "Absolutely. Take your glasses off for a sec, Liz."

Liz obeyed, looking doubtful. Ilana studied Liz's reflection in the mirror with the same look she'd used to appraise Sunita that day in the bathroom. Which seemed like ages ago, Sunita realized wistfully.

"You have so much potential, Liz," Ilana said. "If I were you, I'd pile those red curls in a loose bun on top of your head. And wear green somewhere, to bring out those gorgeous green eyes. Then a pair of classy pearl earrings would really add the finishing touch."

Liz squinted into the mirror intently, and Sunita held her breath.

"Well, okay," Liz said finally. "I'll do it. But only *one* hole in each ear, thank you very much."

Behind Liz's back, Sunita flashed a thumbs-up sign at Ilana. Ilana flashed her a quick smile.

"Hey, I've got a great idea, Ilana!" said Liz suddenly. "Why don't you hang out with us for a while? My mom's picking us up at three, and I'm sure she won't mind giving you a ride home."

Ilana's eyes flickered over to Sunita. For a second, Sunita thought she might accept the invitation. But then she shook her head, making it seem as if the dozens of beaded braids that framed her face were also turning down the offer.

"No, thanks," she said. "I've really got to go. Good luck, Liz."

Sunita felt a pang of regret as she watched Ilana walk gracefully out of the store and disappear into the crowd of shoppers. Would Ilana ever open up to her again?

A salesman with a glint in his eye headed over to the two girls. "Ear piercing for which of you lovely young ladies?" he asked. Sunita pointed to Liz, ignoring her friend's frantic expression.

"It will be over in a second," the man promised.

And it was. Fingering the gold posts in her ears, Liz beamed into the mirror.

"They look great, don't they, Sunni?"

"They look tremendous," Sunita agreed. "Listen, Liz, you go on to the bookstore. I'm going to wander around a bit. I'll come and find you in a while."

Sunita liked strolling through the mall by herself. She bought a soda and sipped it, standing to the side and watching people walk by. Three kinds of people come to shopping malls, she thought. The kind that come to shop, the kind that come to be watched, and the kind that watch the people who come to be watched, like Sunita Sen.

She sauntered along, looking at store windows until a sign caught her eye: New Woman's Beauty Salon. Manicure Special. Five Dollars. Come in with Everyday Hands. Leave with Sheer Glamour.

A little glamour was exactly what she needed. Putting all thoughts of her father's face out of her mind, she headed into the beauty salon.

"A full manicure, please," she told the lady at the front desk.

"The manicurist is right back there, honey," said the lady, pointing to a stall just behind her.

The manicurist was obviously a woman who took her profession seriously. Without a word, she reached for Sunita's left hand and studied it for a minute or two. Sunita watched as her thumbnail took shape under the expert strokes of the manicurist's nail file. She felt hidden and secure in this little stall. I will emerge a new woman, she told herself.

"I need to make an appointment with Irma for Friday afternoon," said a familiar voice on the other side of the divider. It was Mrs. Grayson. Sunita was about to call out and say hello when she heard another familiar voice.

"I hope Sunita's not mad when she sees me, Laurie. I don't know if it was a good idea to let you talk me into coming—"

The lady at the front desk of the beauty salon interrupted. "Please have a seat, ladies. I'll have to call Irma at home."

"It doesn't matter if she's mad, Ranee," said Mrs. Grayson's voice. "The two of you need some mother-daughter time together. Don't worry so much."

"Do I look okay? It feels great to wear slacks again."

"You always look great, Ranee," answered Mrs.

Grayson. "I still don't know why you had to change out of your saree."

"Sunita hates to see me in sarees. But my mother would faint if she saw me in slacks. She's already lectured me several times about how westernized the children are turning out."

Sunita was listening so intently that she hardly noticed when the manicurist reached for her right hand.

"I just don't know what to do about that girl of mine, Laurie." Sunita winced as her mom's voice broke. "My only comfort is that she seems to like spending time with my father. But she's so distant and cold with me."

Sunita heard her mom blowing her nose. So nose blowing was an inherited thing, she thought randomly. "You need to take care of yourself, Ranee, and quit worrying so much about everybody else. Otherwise, you're going to have to ask your parents to leave—I'm not sure you can stand the strain much longer," Mrs. Grayson was saying.

"I don't want them to leave, Laurie," said Sunita's mom. "It's so good to have them here. I guess there's enough Indian still in me to want to make them happy. But I'm not the same obedient daughter that left India all those years ago. I don't know if I *can* make them happy and proud anymore."

"Maybe you're underestimating them," said Mrs. Grayson. "Maybe you need to let them see the lovely, talented woman you've become. Let them be proud of her instead of some ideal Indian daughter you're making up in your head."

Good going, Mrs. Grayson! Sunita thought, silently cheering her on.

"You don't know my mother," answered Sunita's mom, sounding doubtful.

"What about your job? I still think you were crazy to leave it. Any chance you can teach next semester?" Mrs. Grayson was really on a roll now.

"Funny you should bring that up," Mom was saying. "Dr. Thomas called yesterday and practically begged me to teach a couple of classes in January." There was a pause. "I know, I know, Laurie. Don't give me that look. I turned him down."

"For what? So that Ranee Sen, the Ideal Indian Woman, Untouched by Western Sin, can spend all her waking hours waiting on her family hand and foot?" Sunita grinned, realizing that Mrs. Grayson sounded just like Liz when Liz lectured Sunita about something.

"Mrs. Grayson," interrupted the beauty salon lady. "Irma says that three o'clock on Friday is her only free slot. Is that okay?"

"That's fine, thanks. There's a mall rest room just outside, Ranee. Let's go fix your face. We have to meet the girls in a few minutes. Now, as I was saying . . ."

Sunita heard their heels clicking out of the beauty salon. When the door swung shut behind them, she looked down at her hands for the first time. And almost fell out of her chair.

Ten gleaming, pointed, bright-red ovals shone up at her. These hands were not designed to pull weeds in the back yard. These hands were not created to clutch a pencil and do math problems. These hands were designed to curl around champagne glasses. They were made to blow kisses at handsome men.

"I love them!" she said. The manicurist smiled and took the money Sunita handed her.

When Sunita saw her mom and Mrs. Grayson standing near Macy's, she went up to her mother and put her arms around her.

"I'm so glad you came, Mom," she whispered, inhaling the sweet, faint smell of her mother's perfume.

"I'm glad you're glad" was all that Mom said. The four of them headed off to high tea and enjoyed it just as much as they had every year. And Mom, after one long, curious glance, said nothing at all about Sunita's New Woman hands.

Chapter 20

The day after Tea for Four, Sunita decided to take matters into her own hands. She waited until the afternoon when Mom had gone out grocery shopping and Dad had left for an unexpected meeting in town, seized her chance, and went out to the back yard.

"Dadu," she announced. "I've made some tea. Will you come up and have a cup with me . . . *now*?"

Dadu didn't even blink at the urgency in her voice. "I would be delighted. Permit me to wash my hands and I will join you, as you say here, in 'just a sec.' "

She poured the tea and waited nervously until he came into the kitchen. "A good cup of tea readies the mind for anything," he had told her once. She would see if it worked on him.

He sat down and took a long sip of the steaming

tea. "Ahh, delicious. Making good tea must pass from grandmother to grandchild in some mysterious genetic code. Now then, what is on your mind, Bontu?"

"Mom really misses teaching chemistry, Dadu," Sunita blurted out. "Her department chairman asked her to teach a class or two starting January. But she turned him down."

"Really? Interesting. I was quite surprised to hear that she had taken a year off. I was looking forward to sitting in on her lectures. Did you know she won every chemistry honor in her college—and graduated top of her class?" Dadu smiled, and Sunita knew he was remembering how proud he'd been of his only daughter.

"I know she misses teaching," said Sunita. "She turned down the offer because she's trying to be the perfect Indian woman. And the perfect Indian woman, according to Mom, would never neglect the care of her family for a full-time job."

"In that assumption she is mistaken, Bontu," Dadu said. "For generations, an Indian woman's only responsibility used to be serving her parents, in-laws, husband, and children. I have shamelessly benefited from your grandmother's care for half a century. But times are changing, even in India. Though a woman's family responsibilities are still vital, our women are using their God-given gifts in many new ways."

"Well, somehow Mom's got the idea stuck in her head that you and Didu will feel neglected if she teaches while you're here. That if she does, you might feel coming to America spoiled her for good or something. Now *you* might not think that, but Didu is sort of old-fashioned."

"Don't worry, Bontu. I know how to manage your grandmother," said Dadu. "I've been doing it for fifty years. You leave her to me."

Didu came up the stairs, wiping her eyes with one end of her saree. "Doctor Berry died of cancer," she said. "And it was my idea! I feel like such a murderer."

"Cheer up, darling. The actress who played Doctor Berry wanted too much money. You had to get rid of her," said Dadu. He poured his wife a cup of tea. "But I, too, admired that Doctor Berry. She reminded me of that sophisticated Prithi Banerjee."

"Doctor Berry—and Prithi Banerjee?" asked Didu, looking at her husband in bewilderment.

"Think about it, darling. Not very many women can balance a successful medical career and family responsibilities as Prithi does. Take our Ranee, for example. I don't think she could do it. It's a good thing she decided to turn down that job offer."

"What job offer?" asked Didu.

"Bontu was just telling me that Ranee was offered a highly prestigious position teaching at the university," explained Dadu. "She seems so tired lately, and I think it really would be too much for her. She is a lot older than Prithi, isn't she?"

"Don't be ridiculous," said Didu. "Ranee is just as energetic as she always was. And she's only eleven months older than that skinny Prithi Banerjee— who is turning out to be just as scrawny-looking as her mother. That woman still spends most of her time trying to convince everybody that her daughter outshines *our* Ranee. Nobody believes her, of course."

Dadu sighed. "Of course they don't. Not yet, at least. Ah, well. We just won't worry about the rumors that are certain to spread throughout Calcutta."

"Rumors? What rumors?" asked Didu, frowning.

"Prithi is sure to write and tell her mother that Ranee doesn't have a job," said Dadu innocently. "They are certain to wonder why. A girl who graduated at the top of her class with all sorts of honors. A girl like Ranee without a job in the land of opportunity. But we won't pay any attention to their silly gossip, will we, Ria?"

He was good, Sunita thought. He was really good. She looked over at her grandmother hopefully, but Didu seemed to have stopped listening to her husband's gloomy predictions. She was gazing thoughtfully off into space.

"Why in the world would Ranee turn down that offer?" Didu asked, as if to herself. "Teaching is in her blood, after all. Her own father was a brilliant teacher for over forty years. Anyone can see how much she misses it."

Dadu sighed. "I can understand how she feels. I often miss teaching myself," he said.

Sunita looked at him, surprised. He seemed to have temporarily forgotten his reverse-psychology strategy for managing Didu.

"Maybe she doesn't know how proud you are that she followed in your footsteps," Didu said. "I think you should tell her."

Mom walked in, balancing several bags of groceries. "Is this a convention or something?" she asked, putting the bags on the table and looking around at the faces of her parents and her daughter.

"Sit down, Ranee," Dadu said. Mom sat down.

"We heard you turned down a job offer at the university, darling," he said.

Mom glanced suspiciously at Sunita, who tried to look innocent. "How did you hear about that? Yes, I turned it down. I have too much to do around here to teach two classes. Let's drop it, okay?"

Didu ignored Mom's request. "You turned it down?" she asked. "How could you do such a thing?"

Sunita's mom looked at Didu in dismay. "But, Ma," she said. "You always taught that a good Indian woman takes care of her family's needs first—"

"That does not mean that we have the right to

waste our talents and education. Look at Prithi Banerjee. She seems to handle her job and her family quite well. You should take this offer, Ranee. Especially with me here to help you run the house."

"This is a surprise," said Sunita's mom, looking slightly dazed. "Father, what do you think?"

"I would be delighted to visit your classes," he said. "Do you know how proud it makes me feel to know that my daughter has selected teaching as her profession? It is a dream come true for me."

Sunita's mom smiled at Dadu. "I knew you were proud, Father. But you've never told me that before. It's good to hear it. Especially now."

Sunita looked at her grandmother with new respect. So that's what happens after fifty years of marriage, she thought. You manage each other.

"Can you ring this gentleman up and tell him you've changed your mind?" Dadu asked.

"I suppose so," said Sunita's mom. "Maybe I should. First Arun, then Laurie Grayson, and now both of you are telling me the same thing." She turned to her daughter. "Bontu, what do you think?"

Sunita poured another cup of tea and handed it to her mother. "A good cup of tea readies the mind for anything," she said. "Drink this, Mom, and then go for it."

When Dad got home that night and found out that Mom had taken the job, he insisted on ordering a pizza to celebrate. Her face flushed with excitement, Mom described Dr. Thomas's delight over her acceptance. As they listened, Dadu's eyes gleamed behind his glasses, and Didu had to blow her nose loudly every now and then.

Watching them, Sunita suddenly felt that same choked-up feeling she used to get watching Bogart and Bergman in *Casablanca*.

She got up and stood behind her grandfather, put her arms around him, and dropped a kiss on the top of his silvery head. Then she planted a kiss on her grandmother's cheek. It was the first time she'd kissed them since her mom had stopped reminding her to.

Her parents were staring at her in amazement. She hurried out of the room, embarrassed by her own outburst of affection. Sunita's dad broke the astonished silence.

"Teenagers," he said softly, almost reverently. It was like a benediction.

Chapter 21

After Thanksgiving weekend, things changed around the Sen house. Mom spent less time in the kitchen and more time in front of the computer, preparing her course outlines. Didu reigned supreme in the kitchen and even began experimenting with some American recipes. Her attempts at spaghetti, enchiladas, chicken pot pie, and tuna casserole always tasted faintly of curry powder.

Dadu's work in the garden had become less demanding as the days grew colder. One afternoon, Sunita came home from school to find him dressed and waiting for her. He had started wearing an old-fashioned hat to keep his head warm. With his cane, his hat, and a woolen shawl, he looked as if he'd stepped out of a Dickens novel.

"Will you accompany me on a stroll to the library, Bontu?" he asked.

The public library was a prime after-school hang-out. Sunita made up a flimsy excuse about homework. Dadu looked disappointed, but he lifted his hat and left without her.

Sunita's mom wandered into the room.

"Your birthday's coming up soon, Bontu—" she said, and caught herself. "Sorry. I mean Sunita."

Sunita looked embarrassed. "That's okay, Mom," she said. "You can call me Bontu."

"Thanks, Bontu. I can hardly believe that my youngest is turning fourteen. What should we do for a party this year?"

Every year since they had moved into the neighborhood, Mom had thrown a big birthday bash for Sunita. She went all out to make it special. The kids who came talked about it for days afterward.

"I don't want a party this year, Mom," Sunita said.

"Why not?"

"I'm too old for kiddie parties. Besides, I can't have boys over, remember?"

It was Mom's turn to look embarrassed. "That rule is hereby revoked," she said. "It was a dumb one, anyway."

"One of the dumbest," agreed Sunita, grinning.

"So we'll have a co-ed party. It'll be fun with the whole family here too."

Sunita thought quickly. "Planning a party wears us all out, and you're already so busy preparing for your new classes," she said.

Mom looked at her thoughtfully. "If you don't want a party, Bontu, we won't have one," she said.

Sunita felt relieved and disappointed at the same time. She loved having her birthday so close to Christmas. It was a great time for a party, with so many people celebrating peace and love and brotherhood and all that wonderful stuff. This year would seem empty without one. But she certainly couldn't make it through a party that included friends from school, Sunita Sen, *and* her grandparents. She pictured Dadu interrupting a steamy rock video to deliver a lecture on the evils of the American entertainment industry. She imagined her classmates politely trying to dance to sitar music with Didu watching, beaming, and tapping her foot. She'd never make it alive through an evening like that.

On the first day of Christmas vacation, Traci took Liz and Sunita to the mall.

"Meet me by the fountain at five o'clock sharp," said Traci, watching her reflection in the wall of mirrors near the mall entrance. She flicked a tiny piece of lint off her black wool dress and walked off without saying good-bye.

The mall was crowded with tired-looking mothers and grouchy-looking kids waiting in the long line to sit on Santa's lap.

"Let's go watch the ice skaters," said Liz casually.

"Why, Elizabeth Anne Grayson," Sunita teased, "since when did you develop such an overwhelming interest in figure skating? Or is there one figure in particular that you want to watch?"

Liz grinned. "Bill did mention that he and Michael and a bunch of the other kids would be ice-skating today."

They stepped into the viewing balcony that hung over the ice-skating rink. Liz leaned over the railing and waved. A tall, lanky figure that had been peering up at the viewing balcony waved back and immediately started skating backward.

"He's showing you his stuff," said Sunita, giggling and nudging her friend.

Liz watched, entranced, as Bill tried to do a spin and crashed into a little girl, who fell down and started screaming. Bill picked up the kid, dusted her off, handed her some gum from his pocket, and sent her sniveling off to her mother.

"He's so compassionate, isn't he?" murmured Liz. Sunita rolled her eyes.

The music changed, the lights dimmed. A flash of red glided out into the middle of the rink. A blond ponytail tied with a gold ribbon gleamed in the soft gold spotlight. Golden girl herself, thought Sunita. LeAnn Schaeffer. Sunita's eyes searched the rest of the rink. At one end, Michael, Kevin Chang, and a couple of other guys were trying some jumps.

Although Michael had been friendly since their talk in the garden, he hadn't asked her to spend any time with him outside of school. He seemed to be waiting for her to invite him over. He'd even dropped hints about it.

"Any change in regulations?" he'd asked once.

Sunita realized that she couldn't use Mom as an excuse anymore—not since the "no boys" rule had been revoked.

Michael looked up and waved at Sunita and Liz. Then he turned and watched LeAnn do a perfect jump. He applauded along with the others, and she skated toward him, her skirt flaring around her legs.

"Let's go, Liz," Sunita said. "I don't want to waste my time admiring LeAnn."

They headed over to the stationery store. Sunita bought a calligraphy pen and some paper that was bordered with an Indian-style pattern. She had finished writing the final version of her story about Dadu, and she wanted to give it to him for Christmas. The girls finished their shopping at four and sat wearily near the fountain to wait for Traci.

"We've got an hour till she comes. How much money do you have left?" asked Liz, eyeing the ice-cream store. "Shopping always makes me hungry."

"Everything makes you hungry." Sunita rummaged through her purse. "Exactly thirty-two cents," she answered.

"Hey, there's Bill and Michael right over there," said Liz. "Let's go borrow some money from them. Or maybe we can talk them into treating."

Sunita turned to where Liz was pointing. Sure enough, there was Michael. He and Bill were gazing at the window display of a sporting goods store, oblivious to the world around them. Standing nearby, snickering and pointing, stood LeAnn, Jeannie, and a bunch of the other kids. And then Sunita caught a glimpse of what they were pointing at.

Her grandfather. Standing under a big plastic candy cane, dressed in his finest dhoti, with his walking cane hooked over his elbow. He was studying a map of the mall, and Sunita was close enough to see that he looked hot and tired. Shoppers pushed past him, and the map fluttered to the ground. Slowly, he bent over and picked it up again.

"He looks lost, Sunni," said Liz.

Sunita pulled her friend back. "Stay here, Liz," she commanded.

She looked over at the group of her classmates. John Rostowski had wrapped a girl's scarf around himself. He was hunched over, and as she watched, he pretended to mop his forehead with a handkerchief and wring it out. She glanced quickly at her grandfather. Sure enough, he was mopping his forehead with his handkerchief.

She took a step back. In a minute, he was sure to look up and spot her. "Hello, Bontu," he'd call, and wave. "Just doing a bit of shopping." And her classmates' heads would turn toward Sunita.

It was like a scene from a movie. As Sunita watched, the music of "We Three Kings of Orient Are" started playing in the background. Dadu stopped a burly security officer. Sunita had never seen so clearly just how small and thin Dadu was. The officer's big back obscured him from her view.

"Speak up, man. Can't hear a word you're saying," the man said, sounding impatient.

Dadu raised his voice over the piped-in music. "Where might I purchase one of those blank writing books, sir?" Sunita winced as his heavily accented English sounded throughout the area.

"Sorry, buddy, but I don't speak-o no Spanish-o." Shrugging, the man moved on.

What in the world did Dadu want with a blank book? With a flash of insight, Sunita realized he was shopping for her birthday present.

And then she heard LeAnn Schaeffer's giggle. And LeAnn Schaeffer's voice, loud enough for everyone around to hear. "Classy, isn't he?" she said. "Actually, I feel kind of sorry for him. Isn't he a bit too old for diapers?"

Afterward, Sunita didn't remember walking toward LeAnn, grabbing her elbow, and spinning her around.

"Your eyes were really narrowed, Sunni," Liz told her later, sounding awed. "I'd read about 'narrowed eyes' and 'clenched teeth,' but I'd never seen them before."

Sunita stared at LeAnn for a few seconds. "That happens to be my grandfather, LeAnn Schaeffer," she said. "And he has more class in his little finger than you'll ever have in your entire life. I feel sorry for *you*."

Sweeping past her classmates, she walked up to her grandfather and tapped him on the shoulder. Liz followed her, juggling their shopping bags and purses.

"Permit me to assist you, Dadu," Sunita said.

"Bontu!" he said, his face lighting up with pleasure. "What a delightful surprise. And Elizabeth! Just when I was hoping to find an excuse to purchase an ice-cream cone."

Offering an arm to each girl, he led them into the ice-cream parlor. Liz and Dadu stood in line for the ice-cream cones, and Sunita slipped into an empty booth. Through the glass window, she could still see her classmates clustered together in a group. Jeannie had an arm around LeAnn, and she and several other girls were nodding their heads, listening as LeAnn talked. Sunita caught a glimpse of LeAnn's angry, tear-stained face. Suddenly, Sunita's knees felt shaky, and she leaned her head on her arms.

You had nothing to lose, Sunita Sen. You were already a social reject, she told herself. Pull yourself together.

"Mind if I join you?"

Michael slid into the booth next to her without waiting for her answer.

"So that's your grandfather, Sunni," he said. "He doesn't seem so intimidating. What is it that you call him?"

"I call him Dadu. Liz does too. And he's wonderful. Not that your friend LeAnn Schaeffer would ever see that."

"Don't be too hard on LeAnn, Sunni. She gets all those dumb attitudes from her mom. Mrs. Schaeffer's my mom's best friend, but she really exasperates Mom sometimes."

"Did LeAnn send you over here as her defense lawyer or something?"

Michael took a deep breath, as though he was trying to hold on to his patience. "No, Sunni, she didn't," he said slowly. "But I try to defend her when I can. We grew up together, you know, and she's kind of like a sister."

It was amazing how three little words could cheer a person up. *Like a sister.* They had a nice ring to them. Sunita smiled.

But Michael had something else on his mind. "So you didn't want me to meet your grandfather," he said.

"It wasn't that, Michael. It was Mom's rule. I told you about it, remember?"

"I know your mom, Sunni. If you'd really wanted me to come over, you could have talked her into it. But you thought I couldn't handle it, right?"

"No, Michael," she said. Her voice had dropped so low that he had to put his head right next to hers to hear it. "It's that my family is so different from yours. I didn't think you'd like me anymore."

"Listen, Sunita Sen. I'm only going to say this once. All of those differences make you even more fascinating," he said softly. "Especially to me."

She looked up at him. "Really?" she asked.

"Really," he answered. "Who else in our school has a grandfather that looks exactly like Mahatma Gandhi?"

They smiled at each other. Suddenly, Michael pulled away, stood up, and tucked in the back of his shirt. Her grandfather was walking over to them, balancing three ice-cream cones, his slow, loving smile lighting up his whole face.

"Dadu, this is my friend Michael Morrison," she said, after the ice-cream cones had been distributed. Behind Liz, Bill cleared his throat, and Liz poked Sunita with her elbow. "Oh. And this is my friend Bill McTaggart," Sunita added.

Dadu shook their hands courteously. Then they all crowded into the booth.

"Do either of you boys play this sport called base-ball?" he asked.

"They both do, Dadu," answered Liz. "Bill's the starting shortstop and Michael plays first base."

The boys tried to look modest. "Why do you ask, sir?" asked Bill. Sunita stared at him. She'd never dreamed that Bill McTaggart could sound so polite.

"I am going through furious withdrawals from my country's sport of choice—cricket. I need a new sport upon which to focus my attention. I have selected baseball as this sport. But I need to understand it first. Perhaps I may attend some of the baseball matches that you will play?"

Interrupting each other, Bill and Michael started an energetic description of the sport that took over their lives every spring. Dadu began taking notes on his napkin.

Sunita caught Liz's eye and whispered, "Thanks, Aunty Liz."

"For what, silly?" Liz whispered back. "I got my ice-cream cone, didn't I?"

Chapter 22

"I changed my mind, Mom," Sunita said, bursting in through the front door with Liz at her heels. "I do want a birthday party. Is it too late?"

"Bontu! Your birthday's the day after tomorrow!" Mom said.

"I know," Sunita answered. "Just a small party, Mom. Please."

Sunita's mom grinned. "Which of course will include some boys," she said.

"Just a few. I don't want to overwhelm the family by inviting all my boyfriends home at once."

"Sit down, then, girls. We have to do some major planning."

"Who should we invite, Sunni?" Liz asked.

They put several names on the list and took turns calling them on the phone. Most of the kids sounded excited about the party. "We were sad you weren't going to have one this year, Sunni," several of them told her.

"Anyone else?" Liz asked, chewing on her fingernails. Despite Mrs. Grayson's cooperation, none of Liz's nails had made it through her observation experiment.

Sunita thought for a moment. "Just one person," she said. Taking a deep breath, Sunita dialed Ilana Taylor's number. She didn't really know why she was even trying. Ilana would probably turn the invitation down, sounding as cool and reserved as she always did.

A funny-sounding voice answered the phone. "Hed-do?" it said.

"Is Ilana there?" asked Sunita.

"Thid id Idada," said the voice. "I have a terrible code. Who id thid?"

Sunita was taken aback for a minute. Could Ilana Taylor, the queen of eighth-grade poise and sophistication, actually have a stuffy nose? It didn't compute. But it did help Sunita relax.

"It's me, Sunni," she said. "I've just decided to have a birthday party day after tomorrow, and I was hoping you'd come. That is, if you feel up to it."

There was no answer, which was much more encouraging than the instant rejection Sunita had anticipated. Maybe if she kept talking, she could convince Ilana to come.

"It might even cure your cold," she said, thinking desperately. "You know, starve a cold, feed a fever. Uh—I mean feed a cold and starve a fever. Anyway, you'll get to eat the tons of Indian food that my grandmother's already started to cook. The spices alone will clear your sinuses right away. And my grandfather knows all kinds of great home remedies. My sister had a wart once—"

"Wade a sec," interrupted Ilana. She blew her nose. "Ahh. That's better. Did you say your grandparents will be there? Are they the ones you wrote about in your social studies essay?"

"Yes, that's them. They're staying with us for a while."

"I guess I'll come then. I'd love to meet them. What time should I be there?"

Sunita hung up, feeling slightly dazed by the unexpected turn of events. But she couldn't spend too much time ruminating on them. She had way too much to do.

She and Liz stayed up late two nights in a row planning the activities for the evening—eating and games and talking first, and then videos and dancing after all the people over twenty were safely upstairs for the night. Mom and Didu stayed up with them, sautéeing, baking, simmering, frying, roasting, and steaming all sorts of delicacies.

On the day of the party, Liz arrived early to help decorate. Geetie ran to the store to buy environmentally safe paper cups and plates. Dad mowed the lawn. Dadu bought huge bunches of flowers from the local farmers' market and gave them to Didu, who made bouquets and filled every vase in the house.

Later, Sunita caught her grandfather going from vase to vase, adding something to each bouquet. When she looked closer, she saw that they were clippings from the plants that she had grown in the good soil during her observation experiment. They were still flourishing, mainly because she had continued to water them even after the end of the semester.

"Didu's arrangements look so beautiful already, Dadu. Why are you adding those?" she asked.

He tucked a clipping into her hair. "Here you are, my dear," he said. "I thought we could present these as a birthday gift to the Sunita Sen who will thrive and grow in the years to come. They are the promise of the lovely result when good soil and a faithful gardener become partners."

With a smile, he hurried off to don a crisply ironed dhoti before the first guests arrived. Didu put on her nicest saree.

"We want to impress your friends so they will come back," she told Sunita and Liz. "We have missed having hordes of children around. In Calcutta, the neighborhood children all congregate at our house."

When the kids arrived, they did seem impressed.

Especially Ilana, who couldn't take her eyes off Didu's shimmering silk saree. Dadu shook hands with all of them before handing them a plate, which Didu proceeded to load with food. After a huge five-course dinner, the kids fell groaning onto the big pillows in the Sens' family room.

"I can't move," complained Bill, clutching his stomach. "I'll never be able to waste Liz in the two-mile again."

"Waste me? You just barely beat me, McTaggart, and you know it!"

"Okay, okay, you two," interrupted Michael. "We've heard this conversation at least three hundred times."

Kevin Chang turned to Sunita, who was sprawled on her favorite pillow. "What do you call those beautiful outfits your mom and grandmother are wearing, Sunni?" he asked.

Liz answered before Sunita could. "That's a saree, Kev. And I'm going to wear one someday. After all, Sunita's grandfather always says I'm an honorary Indian."

Dadu came down the stairs just in time to overhear her. "You are indeed, Elizabeth," he said. "And with those flaming curls and flashing green eyes, you would be a stunning sight in a royal green saree."

He turned to Ilana and bowed slightly. "And you, my dear, have the grace and stature that was designed for the flowing lines of a saree," Dadu said.

176

"Let's try some on right now, Sunni," said Liz, carried away by Dadu's description.

"They look so exotic," added Ilana.

Sunita shrugged. "My grandmother's the saree expert. I'll ask her to help us."

Bill sighed. "Since we're not going to get dessert for a while, let's play some Ping-Pong, guys."

"You're on, McTaggart," Michael said. Leaning closer to Sunita, he added softly, "Why don't you put one on too, Sunni? I'd love to see you in one of those things."

"May I join you fellows?" asked Dadu. "I used to play quite a bit of table tennis in my college days. We will wait for the ladies to burst in on us in their splendor."

The girls clattered upstairs to ask Didu if she would help them try on sarees. For a moment, Sunita caught a glimpse of the smile that must have captured Dadu's heart years ago.

"The saree has a great advantage over dresses," Didu told them, rummaging through her closet. "How do you say it in this country? Ah yes . . . one size fits all."

One by one, Didu held up sarees in front of each girl.

"This color is just right for you, Liz. Ilana, hold up this blue one." Shifting easily from English into Bengali, she turned to her granddaughter. "Why don't you go in your mother's room to get the purple and gold saree I brought for you from India?"

One by one, the girls stood patiently as she draped, pleated, and tucked the long pieces of silk around them. Then she opened another box, and they gasped at the gold and jewels that sparkled inside.

"Help yourselves, girls," said Didu grandly.

They draped themselves with bangles, necklaces, and earrings, and then trooped into Mom's room to take turns admiring themselves in the full-length mirror. Sunita's turn came last, and she turned slowly in front of the mirror. The saree definitely made her look older. It even made her look as though she had some curves.

"I'm going down, Sunni," said Liz impatiently. Sunita grinned. Her friend couldn't wait to dazzle Bill with all her finery.

Didu came over to admire her granddaughter.

"How do I look?" Sunita asked her.

Didu thought for a moment. "You look . . . let me see . . . entirely chilly . . . no, no, that's not right, is it? Aha! Don't tell me—you look . . . totally cool, darling," answered Didu, pinching Sunita's cheek tenderly. Sunita planted a kiss on her grandmother's cheek.

She is the last one to go down the stairs. Dadu and the boys are busy admiring the other girls at the far end of the room, but Michael is looking up, waiting for her. Slowly, she glides down, her golden bangles clinking together in melodious, graceful accompaniment.

"You look . . . just like I thought you would, Sunni," he whispers when she reaches him. "Are you sure you're still Sunita Sen and not some exotic Indian princess coming to cast a spell on me?"

"I'm sure, Michael," she tells him, giving him one of her trademark smiles just to prove it.